LUKE

SUSIE MCIVER

BOOK 9

IN THE BAND OF NAVY SEALS

AUTHOR

SUSIE MCIVER

This is a work of fiction. Names, characters, organizations, places, events, and incidents are either products of the author's imagination or are used fictitiously.

Text copyright 2021 Susie McIver

All rights reserved.

No part of this book may be reproduced, or stored in a retrieval system, or transmitted in any form or by any means, electronic, mechanical, photocopying, recording, or otherwise, without express written permission of the author.

Cover Design by Emmy Ellis

❀ Created with Vellum

1

LUKE

*L*uke Wilson's life ended four years ago when his wife, Susan, died on a mission overseas. He tried everything to get her to leave with him, but she stayed behind. Nothing he said would make her change her mind. They argued over it, Susan was a nurse, and she thought she was needed where she needed to stay where she was. No matter what he said? Luke was being deployed to another place. He was a Navy Seal, and he went where his lieutenant told him to go. He had to leave. That was the last time he saw his wife. They had a huge argument, and he couldn't tell her he was sorry.

Luke's life was a crazy one. He acted like he didn't give a damn about his life since he left the Navy Seals. He and his Harley traveled the American roads for four years. He went all over the United States. He's been barely existing. He hasn't kept count of the women he's been with, but nothing took away the memory of the last argument he had with his wife. He felt like he should have done more to get Susan to leave with him. He didn't know what he could have done.

But he should have done something to make her leave with him. He felt responsible for her death.

Lieutenant Killian Cooper called and asked him to join a security guard business called Band of Navy Seals. Luke thought about it for over a month before he called him back and joined the Band of Navy Seals team. Luke couldn't keep doing what he was doing, and it felt good being around his buddies again. He had let his hair grow, he stopped smiling. He didn't care anymore about his life. But being around his friends he felt like maybe his life was getting better. He knew his friends were surprised by how much he'd changed, not just his looks but his personality. Luke didn't care if he lived or died when he first got here. It's been so long since he's tried to smile.

That was over a year ago, and it was the first time he met the beautiful Missy Devlin. When he gazed into her eyes, something slammed into his heart. He knew he wanted her like he's never in his life wanted woman. The need he felt went straight to his cock. Not even Susan made his body acting like this. It made him feel guilty for feeling the he did. Her red hair curled around her beautiful face. He wanted to put his fingers in her hair and pull her to him for hot kiss. Her blue-gray eyes felt like they pierced right through him, straight to his heart. She was tall. The top of her head came to his chin. All he would have to do was bend his head and capture her lips with his. There was something about her that had him taking a step toward her at the same time she stepped toward him. But one of the team stepped between them.

MISSY DEVLIN WAS A PEOPLE PERSON. She had lots of friends but sometimes she felt alone. She had a mind for making money, and she always let her friends in on her adventures. Missy knew Luke wasn't someone she should get involved with, and she told herself she wouldn't. He would break her heart. But when her eyes gazed into his, she fell in love. One look, and she knew. Her friends knew she had fallen in love. She told them she loved him. They all thought she was crazy. Luke carried all that pain in his eyes, and Missy wanted to see if she could help ease that pain or take it away. She knew she wouldn't act on that thought. She didn't want a broken heart. So she kept away from him as much as she could. He told her once they would make hot passionate love together, and that is why she stayed away. She knew it would be forever for her, but just another woman in bed for Luke.

Her friend, Julia, and the others told her he would just break her heart. So why did Missy feel like her heart was already broken? She was confused because she had never felt like this. For more than a year, her friends had managed to be around while Luke was in the same room as she was. So they never got to enjoy that hot passionate sex. They were friends, but not close friends. They never talked alone or about personal stuff. They were friends who nodded their heads to each other and said hey in passing.

LUKE SAW IT ALL UNFOLD. He was too far away to save her. He and Austin were on their way to Missy's house. She lived close to Kane and Julia's in Montana.

Missy was jumping from rock to rock. There was a light dusting of snow that covered the ground. She hopped on one that was slippery, and when she fell into the icy river, she hit her head on the rock, and it knocked her out. Luke was running and shouting for Harold to save her.

Harold saw everything. He ran along the bank, shouting

for help. "Jump in and save her, Harold! Jump in before she gets to the rapids. Do it now," Albert, Harold's dead brother, shouted.

"But what if you go away? I won't be able to see you anymore," Harold cried.

"I'll always be here with you. Do it!"

Harold jumped in the raging water. He swam as hard as he could to reach Missy. He reached out and grabbed her foot as she went past him. He caught her before she hit the rapids. He pulled her around and lifted her head above the water. He gave all he had to reach the bank. He pulled her out and turned her over. Then Luke took over.

"Come on, sweetheart, wake up." Luke worked until Missy vomited water and started coughing. "Hey, Missy, can you open your eyes?"

Missy opened her eyes and looked around. She vomited up more water. She spotted Harold with water running down his face. She turned her head and saw Luke. His face was chalk white. "Thank you, both. Harold, I know how hard it had to be for you to jump into the river. Are you alright?"

"Albert yelled at me to jump in, so I did. Are you going to be okay?"

"Yes, thanks to you, I'll be fine. Can you tell Albert I said thank you? Are you going to be able to talk to him anymore?" Missy's teeth were clattering. She was freezing, and so was Harold; she could see him shaking. His lips were turning blue.

"He said he would always be around. I can talk as much as I want to him. He will always hear me. It was my fault Albert died. He told me to stay off the ice because it wasn't frozen enough to ice skate on. He stayed under me until I got out of the water. He didn't make it out of the freezing water. And he never left me. He talks to me all the time. I just didn't want him to go away."

LUKE

Luke held Missy in his arms. He reached over and pulled a scared fifteen-year-old boy into his arms as well. The three of them sat there holding each other.

Luke pulled them up and looked at Austin. "Come on, we have to get them inside and warm them up. Missy will have to have that injury looked at."

"I don't think I can walk," Missy said, looking at Luke. He picked her up and took off walking. Austin threw Harold over his shoulder and followed. Missy told Luke where to go. Her room was on the ground floor. And Austin helped Harold upstairs to the other suite.

"Luke, can you please help me get this jacket off."

Luke unzipped her jacket and helped her out of it. Then he pulled her top over her head. His hands stilled as he saw the scars on her back. He knew someone had beaten her. Why hadn't he known this about Missy? He didn't realize he was touching them. He bent his head to kiss away the pain when she spoke.

"It's okay, Luke. They're just scars, they don't hurt anymore," she whispered.

He pulled her snow pants off, and then he started her shower. The water was warm. Luke carried Missy into the shower and held on to her as her body got warm. Missy kept her head on his shoulder as the tears fell down her face.

"Why are you crying?" he whispered.

"Albert's gone."

Luke inhaled slowly. He knew his body was betraying him. But there wasn't anything he could do about that. He has wanted to be naked with Missy since he laid eyes on her, and over the year, the feelings became stronger.

"Sweetheart, Albert's been gone."

"But not for Harold. Now he won't be back."

"Maybe that's a good thing. Are you ready to get out? I

don't think I can stand here another second without getting naked with you."

"Yes, I'm ready. This is the first conversation I've had with you."

"We both know why we've stayed apart, and I'm not going to discuss that with you right now."

"I'll get something of Zane's for you to wear," Missy said, wrapping a housecoat around her. She stepped into her closet and stripped her bra and undies off.

Missy went into Zane and Aunt Polly's room they used when they were here and got some clothes for Luke and some sweats and a T-shirt for Harold. She set them on the bed for Luke, and she gave Austin Harold's clothes. Then she got herself something to wear. Her head was spinning. She looked in the mirror. It really wasn't much of a cut. She thought she would be okay not to go to the hospital.

Luke walked into the kitchen and saw Missy sitting there. "We are ready to take you to the hospital."

"I don't think I need to go to the hospital."

"Then I'll stay here with you."

"Alright, let's go. Harold, I will never be able to thank you enough for saving my life."

"I'm thankful I was here with you. So I could save your life. You shouldn't jump on the rocks. It's too dangerous."

"I'll remember that. Believe me, I'll never jump on the rocks again. Are you sad because Albert's gone?"

"I am sad. But Albert needed to go. He's been with me a long time. Now he can be with other people and help them."

"You are so giving and smart. I wish I'd had a brother like you."

"Thank you. I can be your brother."

"Will you be my brother?"

"Yes."

"Missy threw her arms around him. Thank you."

"The hospital said Missy had a concussion, but she was going to be okay. She promised Luke she would stay at Julia's for the night. That's where they dropped her off.

"I SWEAR, Julia, when he held me in that shower, I thought for sure we were going to end up in bed together. I really believe if Austin and Harold weren't there, then we would have. I knew that wouldn't be a good idea. Because if I had made love with Luke, I would never want to let him go."

"I'm glad Austin was there too. Tell me about Harold. If Harold or Luke hadn't been there, you would have died."

"I know. That's so scary. Harold said he would be okay. He told me Albert could help other people now that he wasn't with him all the time. Isn't he amazing?"

"He really is. I love that kid."

"I know. Harold said Albert told him to jump in and save me. I think I'll miss Albert a lot. I swear it felt like he drowned, and I'm so damn sad over that. Isn't that crazy? I liked hearing all the things he told Harold."

"No, I don't think it is crazy at all. I think we will all miss Albert. I'm glad Harold is okay. Tell me what you're going to do about Luke?"

"I really don't know what to say. He saw my scars, and those ugly things didn't seem to bother him. I had to tell him they didn't hurt anymore. I felt like he was angry at seeing them more than anything."

"I told you they aren't that bad. I'm sure Luke wanted to murder the bastard who did that to you. That was my feeling when I saw them."

"Was it? Oh, brother, you're going to have me crying."

Julia smiled at Missy, "Of course, I was angry. You're my best friend; I wanted to kill the person who hurt you."

"I swear, Julia, I'm so blessed to have you as my best friend."

Julia hugged her. "I want you to be more careful on those rocks. You should see if there is something you can put on them, so they aren't slippery."

"Oh yeah, like what? I didn't know there was anything available to put on them."

"You should ask Piper. She would know."

"You're right. I'll call her."

2

Luke was with Zane. They were transporting two boys from Afghanistan to their grandfather in America. Luke wanted to ask him how Missy got those damn scars. He knew someone had to have beaten her with a strap. He also knew if he asked Zane, he better be prepared to listen to a lecture. Or a hard fist coming at his face. Everyone on the Seal team watched over Missy, but Zane was her uncle by marriage. Luke didn't care. He had to know who did this to her."

He took a deep breath and looked over at Zane. "How did Missy get those scars on her back?"

"I wondered when you would ask me that question. When Missy was seventeen, she was kidnapped by a man who was her teacher. Missy had become involved with the guy. It was a brief thing, very brief. He took advantage of her after her grandma died. She thought he was more a father figure which she never had. Her parents died when she was toddler. When Missy tried stopping it, the man went ballistic and kidnapped her. He raped her and beat her unconscious. She was missing for two weeks. Polly hired us to guard Missy after she was out of the hospital. The guy is already dead. He had a wife, and his son was a senior in the same school. The teacher committed suicide, his wife was so distraught she committed suicide."

"What happened to the son?"

"He joined the army."

"What did that Bastard hit her with?"

"She said he had a horsewhip."

"Bastard, I wish he was alive, so I could kill him."

"Why do you wish that?"

"Hell, I don't know. I just know I was so angry when I saw those scars. You don't have to worry that I'm going to seduce Missy. I don't know why I have this protective instinctive toward Missy, but I do."

"Luke, I know how screwed up you are. I'm going to tell you right now, don't mess with Missy. I don't think she could handle having a broken heart."

"Why the hell do you think I would break her heart? I want to help her as a friend would help a friend."

"I heard about you helping her. Thank you for that. She also told me you saw her scars. I don't mean to offend you either, but my worry is that Missy has always been someone who gives and gives. She never meets a stranger, and that scares me."

"Why does it scare you?"

"Because she welcomes everyone into her life and I don't know where Shawn is. She could befriend someone close to him and end up being hurt by him. He's the teacher's berserk son. We've been keeping an eye on him. He was kicked out of the Army for raping two women and beating them. He went to prison for two years, and now we don't know where he is. When he raped and beat those women, he called them Missy."

"Fuck, did you tell her this?"

"No, Polly didn't want me to say anything."

"I think you need to say something right now. If Missy sees the son, she can get the hell away from him. He is deranged and blames Missy for all of their family's problems. Crap, do I have to do everything?"

Luke stood up and walked to the front of the plane. He dialed Missy's number. It sounded like she was out of breath when she answered, and he realized she was probably running.

"Hello."

"Missy, it's Luke. Are you running?"

"Yes. I just finished my ten-mile run. What's up, Luke?"

"Listen, why don't you call me when your run is over?"

"It's okay, I've finished. I'm almost at my car. Tell me."

"I was talking to Zane, and he said they have been keeping track of Shawn Warham. Do you know who he is?"

"Yes. Why is Zane keeping an eye on him?"

Because he went to prison for raping and beating two women. Each woman said he called them Missy, as he was abusing them. Listen, they've lost track of him. I'm going to send you an updated picture of him. I believe he's going to come for you. Go straight to Kane and Julia's house and stay there until we've located this creep."

"No."

"Missy…." *Damn, she hung up on me.* Luke pushed her number into his phone again. "Don't hang up on me."

"I don't want to hear this. Don't you understand? I wondered when he would come after me. I knew he blamed me for everything that happened. Hell, I blamed myself for a while. Until I smartened up and realized it was my teacher who took advantage of me. I'm surprised he hasn't already tried to kill me. Thanks for the heads up. I'll keep my eyes open."

"Shut the hell up. Why won't you listen to me? This guy is

crazy. Go to Kane's until I get there, and then I'll take you away somewhere until we find out where this jerk is. Don't hang up on me. Damn it," he blurted out the last two sentences as he heard the line go dead. He called Julia and explained everything to her. Hopefully, she was able to talk some sense into Missy.

~

Missy hit the steering wheel with the palm of her hand. She had prayed for that part of her life to be over. But now she knew Shawn was hunting for her. He probably already knew where she lived. He was just waiting for the right time to grab her. She had to leave until Zane found out where he was. She called Willow and asked if she could stay at her place in Maine. "Willow, please don't tell anyone where I am. Not even Ash," she said when Willow agreed to let her stay.

"You be careful, Missy. I'm going to ask you to call me every night, so I'll know you're safe. When you don't call, I'll tell Ash where you are. I'll know something is wrong."

"I'll call you, I promise. Thanks, Willow." Missy went home and took a shower. Then she packed a bag, and called a taxi, and went into Kalispell. Missy walked to a used car lot. She had a wig on and a fake I.D. Like she told Luke, she wasn't surprised Shawn would hunt her down. She was prepared to disappear for a while. She got into her new, used car and drove. She called Willow.

"Hey, Willow. I've decided to go somewhere else. I don't want you to have to keep secrets from Ash. I'm also going to throw my phone away. I don't want it to be tracked."

"Give me your new phone number. You can't just disappear without one of us knowing where you are."

"I'm not going to keep the same phone. I'm buying a

burner phone every week. I promise to call you every few days. You can keep me updated on what's going on."

"You are watching way to much CSI shows. Missy, we love you. Let someone help you."

"I love all of you too. I can handle this. I've been preparing for years for Shawn to come after me. Bye, Willow." Missy had to pull over. She was crying so hard. *Damn it, I don't want to do this. I'll go to the Blue Ridge Mountains. I have a cabin there, and no one knows about it except Harold. I told him about it when I bought it in case he needed to tell someone. I'll stay there until Shawn is found.* She had everything she would need in the cabin except food.

She pulled back out onto the freeway and started her drive to North Carolina. An hour later, her wig felt like it was squeezing her head. She pulled over again and took the damn thing off. *I'll put it back on before I get my hotel room.* This was going to be a long trip, and she was going to take her time. She already missed Luke. At least being home, she knew he was close by. *I'm pathetic. Why do I love him?* He doesn't want my love. I don't think he does anyway. He is still hung up on his cheating wife. Dallas Sawyer, Austin's brother, told them Susan was cheating on her husband. When she died, she was walking next to her lover, who stepped on a land mine. He was also married. She hoped no one ever told Luke about his cheating wife. He loved her so much.

That night, she stopped at a motel right off the freeway. She decided she would stay at small motels every night. It was less likely someone would find her in a motel. They were used to her staying in big five-star hotels. She wasn't sure if her friends would look for her or not, but something told her they just might. Okay maybe she did watch to much CSI and FBI shows.

3

*S*hawn was glad to finally arrive in Missy's town. *I know Missy will be around all her friends. I remember she collects friends as fast as a bee finds honey. The people in this town are so excited to talk about the Band of Navy Seals. Like they are so important, I already knew all about them.*

He knew they guarded Missy when his dad tried to kill her. And when the man he hired to kill her and her Aunt attempted to kill them was murdered. He pretended it was his father who hired those men. Shawn had more information than he asked for from the people of this small town. He found Missy's house on the river. Shawn set up a tent on the other side of the river, watching her home. Not one light had come on in the last week. It was time he moved to plan B. He would ask the kid who came there once a week and cleaned up the area. He followed the kid into town, and when he stopped at the hamburger stand, Shawn ordered himself a hamburger to start a conversation. Then he started talking with him.

"Hello, could you help me? I'm trying to find my high

school friend, Missy Devlin. My phone has no bars in these mountains."

"Missy's not home right now."

"Can you tell me where she is?"

"No, I don't know where she is. Missy has other homes. She has one in California and one in Nashville. And she has a cabin."

"Where is the cabin?"

Harold thought he should shut up before he gave anymore information about Missy that he shouldn't give. "I don't know. I can't remember. I mean, she never told me. I keep her yard picked up. She doesn't tell me her business. She's the kindest person I know."

"Yes, Missy has always been kind. Even when she was in grade school, she was kind to everyone," Shawn rolled his eyes. If he had a knife on him, he would stick it in this kid's heart. He hated it when anyone said nice things about Missy. He couldn't help it. He hated Missy, who always had more friends than she knew what to do with. She murdered his family, so he had to murder her.

"I guess she forgot I was coming this month for a visit."

"Missy doesn't usually forget things. She always writes everything down on her phone," Harold said, frowning at the guy. Now he wondered if he should go to the safe house and tell them about the guy asking questions. The more he watched the guy, the more he looked like someone Missy would stay away from. He didn't think this man was friends with Missy. Harold thought he looked like he had evil in him. He always looked at their eyes, and this guy looked like he didn't have a soul.

Harold forgot all about his hamburger. He jumped on his bike and headed to the safe house. He was going to tell the Band of Navy Seals someone was asking questions about Missy.

Harold didn't dare tell the man about Missy's cabin. Harold didn't hear the vehicle as it turned its wheels straight toward him. He felt the car hit him from behind, and he flew into the air. Harold didn't know anything else, as his head hit the vehicle's windshield before he landed in the ditch on the side of the road. Shawn laughed. No one would find that kid for a long time.

Shawn stepped on the gas pedal and got the hell away from the area. He now knew Missy was gone. That's all he needed to know. The kid wouldn't be alive to let anyone know he'd been there asking questions. He needed to make a plan. *How the hell can I find out where Missy is? Think, Shawn, you're smarter than all of them put together.* He had to find out what property she owned. He would bet anything she was at that cabin. He needed to find out where it was.

LUKE WAS on his Harley when he saw the bike in the ditch. *Fuck, Harold's bike.* He pulled over and looked in the ditch on the side of the road. Maybe he was okay and got up and walked away. He saw his leg and ran. Oh, God, don't let him be dead. When Luke reached Harold, he knew it was terrible. There was so much blood. His helmet was lying beside him. His leg was broken for sure, but his head injury was the worst. Luke called nine-one-one. He took his jacket off and laid it on the ground, then he carefully picked Harold's head out of the muddy ditch and laid it on the jacket. He called the safe house and told Riley he needed help. Five minutes later, Ryes, Austin, and Riley pulled up beside his Harley.

"What happened?" Riley cried. She looked at Harold and couldn't stop crying. "He must have been coming back to the safe house. He left earlier today. I wonder why he was coming back."

"Whoever hit him kept going. Look where the tires hit

him. The vehicle must have come off the side of the road in order to hit him. It's almost like they wanted to hit him, like it was intentional. Where is that damn ambulance?"

Ryes began cleaning up the area on Harold's head where he must have hit the person's windshield. "See this glass embedded in his head, he had to have hit the windshield." Ryes could barely feel a heartbeat. He looked at Harold's face, and he wanted to murder whoever did this to him. "We should call his family to meet us at the hospital. His skin is not a good color."

The ambulance showed up at the same time the police did. "What happened?"

Luke was so angry he shook as he looked over at the police officer. "Hit and run. I found Harold on the side of the road. Look at those tire marks. You can get a good imprint of the tire and find out what kind of car that was. Then we can try finding it. I have a friend who can do amazing stuff with tracking."

"I'm not sure if we can do that. I've never made a tire imprint before. How do you figure out what kind of car it is?"

"Do you have any plaster with you?"

"Yes, I have some in my trunk."

"Can you get it for me?"

The policeman brought the plaster and two bottles of water. Luke made the imprint. "Take this to the FBI. They'll tell you what kind of vehicle this imprint belongs to. As soon as you find out call me. I want to know who went off the road just to kill Harold."

"Do you believe this was done on purpose?"

"Of course, it was. Someone wanted to run him over, and I intend to find out who has done this to my young friend."

"Do you think the boy will live?"

"I don't know. He has a nasty head injury. I hope he

makes it through this. Harold doesn't deserve to die like this. But, I've learned in my life that you don't have control over when it's your time to go. I have to leave. I need to get out of these bloodied clothes and get to the hospital."

Missy was tired, so she pulled over to stretch her legs. It was a beautiful day. There was a cool breeze on her face. She saw an ice cream stand and walked over. She bought herself a large vanilla cone. Then she sat on a bench in the park. She was already lonesome. Missy enjoyed talking to her friends, but most of the time, she was alone. She has lots of friends, but they all have their own lives. She decided to call her new brother, Harold. There was no answer. She had already been on the road for five days. She finished her ice cream and decided to get a motel room in this little town.

Then she would call Julia and tell them she was okay. "Hey, Julia, it's me, Missy. I'm calling to tell you I'm fine. I don't want you to worry about me."

"Missy, where are you? I have some sad, sad news. Harold was hit by a car. The person did it on purpose. Luke found him in the ditch on the side of the road."

"What? That's horrible. How is he?"

"He's still in a coma. The doctors don't think he's going to make it. His family won't leave the hospital. It's so sad. What are you doing? Why can't we get a hold of you?"

"Because Shawn is hunting for me. I told you about him. He was always crazy. I don't want to bring him around my friends. I have to hang up. Goodbye, Julia."

"Come home. We can protect you."

"I knew he was going to come after me. I'm prepared for it. Where is Harold at?"

"He's in Kalispell in ICU on the second floor."

"Thank you. Bye."

"Bye," Julia replied reluctantly. She knew Missy would make her way to the hospital. She called Luke and told him about their conversation. "She'll be there probably tomorrow. She didn't say she would, but I know she won't stay away from Harold. You know, the only reason I'm telling you this is because I know Missy needs someone with her. She said that crazy fucker is after her."

"I know. Thanks, Julia."

Luke packed a bag and went to the hospital to wait for Missy. He knew she would come and visit Harold. She loves him like a little brother. He would wait for her.

4

Missy walked into the hospital and looked around. She had on a nurse's uniform, she had a blonde wig on, and she knew no one would recognize her. She looked completely different from the woman with short red hair that curled around her face. She wore flats because she was tall already. Missy didn't want to add to her height. She walked straight to the second floor and to Harold's room. She stopped at the foot of his bed. Tears fell from her eyes.

"Hey, little brother. I want you to wake up. Are you in a lot of pain?"

"He can't feel anything."

Missy looked over at Luke. "How did you know it was me?"

"Come on, Sweetheart, I'd recognize you anywhere."

"Tell me what happened."

"Someone hit him with their car and then left. I believe it was on purpose. The tires went off the road into the bike lane."

"Why would someone do that?"

"I don't know. There are crazy people in this world. He was on his way to the safe house. I'm not sure if he wanted to tell us something or why he wanted to return to the safe house."

"How is he?"

"The doctor said the sooner he wakes up, the better his chances are for a complete recovery." He turned and looked at her, "Do you want to tell me what this is all about? Why did you disappear?"

"Because I don't want anyone to get hurt by helping me. You don't understand how it is with me. I've had people watching over me since this episode in my life happened. Sometimes I feel smothered. I know it's because they worry about me. Hell, I worry about myself. I don't want to die. That's why I'm going away for a while. I don't want Shawn to hurt any of my friends."

"Don't you think you're safer staying here?"

"No. I don't think I would be safer here. I don't want my friends getting hurt."

"Missy, he's just a man. We're better able to keep you safe."

"No."

"Then I'm going with you."

"Nope." Missy was shaking her head. There is no way she wanted Luke with her.

"I didn't ask you, I told you. I already have my stuff here."

"That tells me one thing, Julia called you and told you about our conversation. You guessed I would come and see Harold."

"No, I knew you would come and see Harold. Can we go get a cup of coffee? I haven't had my caffeine for the day."

"Yes." Missy bent and kissed Harold on the forehead. "I'll be back, little brother."

"Okay."

Missy smiled and looked at Luke, who had a grin on his face. "Can you hear me, Harold?"

"Yes. He opened one eye halfway. The other one was swollen shut."

"What happened to me?"

"You were on your bike, and you got hit by a vehicle."

Suddenly, machines were blaring and nurses were filling up the room, one calling for a doctor. One nurse tried to chase them out of the room, but Harold didn't want them to leave. "I remember," Harold rushed, stopping them in their tracks. "It was the same man who talked to me. I saw him when I flew in the air. I was going to tell Luke he was asking questions about you. Why are you wearing a wig?"

"I didn't want anyone seeing me." She looked at Luke. "But Luke recognized me. Do you think that was Shawn who was asking about me?"

"What did he look like?" he asked Harold.

"You two have to leave the room. The doctor is on his way up here right now."

Luke ignored her. He watched Harold as he looked at them. "The guy had dark hair, but it didn't really fit him. I thought he might have died it. But his eyes were..."

"An almost white blue."

"Yes."

The nurse was ushering them out of the room now.

"Harold, I'm so happy you are going to be okay. I love you. Remember that. I have to leave. I'll see you as soon as we catch Shawn."

"Be careful."

"I will," she bent and kissed him goodbye. She took her phone out and called Riley. "Riley, I want to hire the Band to watch over Harold... Can you have someone here within the hour? Thank you." She turned and walked away.

Harold looked at Luke. "Are you going with her?"

"Yes, I'm sure she's going to throw a fit, though. I'll see you around. Take care of yourself."

"I will," his eyes were already closing.

5

Luke picked up his bag and ran after Missy. "Missy, wait. I'm going with you."

Missy stopped and turned around. "Why are you going with me? I have a place to go where no one will find me. I don't need a bodyguard."

"I want to help you. Why can't you just accept it and say thank you?"

"Fine, you can come with me. But don't think you can boss me around."

"I would never think that. How did you get here?"

"A taxi. I bought a car, but it's at another airport."

"Really, I checked all the car lots.

"I used another name."

"Did you have to show ID?"

"Yes, I have a fake ID."

Luke opened the passenger door to his truck, and Missy got in. He got in on his side. "So, do you want to tell me where we are going?"

"Yes, we are going to the Blue Ridge Mountains. I have a cabin there. We'll stop at the airport, and I'll pick up my car."

"Why don't we just use one vehicle? And since we will be going to the Blue Ridge Mountains, I think my truck will be better for climbing the roads in the Blue Ridge."

"Whatever you say. It's a long drive." She looked a bit pensive for a brief moment before she said, "I'm not surprised Shawn found me. He has always blamed me for his mom and dad killing himself before he was caught. I was stupid, and my teacher took advantage of me when my grandma died. I don't blame anyone for that. But his father hurt me, so I'm not going to apologize to anyone. He deserved to die. I would have killed him myself if I had a weapon."

"Have you ever talked to someone about this?"

"Like who?"

"I don't know. A therapist, maybe."

"No. Have you ever talked to anyone about your problem?"

"I don't have a problem."

Missy shook her head. She didn't know why she loved this man. They have been hot for each other since their first meeting. He could make her so angry. She turned in her seat and looked at him. "What do you mean you don't have a problem? Look at yourself. You are always angry. You need someone to talk to. I don't."

"I'm not always angry."

"I'm not going to argue with you. I don't think it will work out with us driving all the way to the Blue Ridge Mountains together. I can see right now you will want to argue the entire way."

"I'm not going to argue, I promise. I just don't know what you mean when you say I'm angry all the time."

"You're kidding, right?"

"No, I'm not. When have you seen me angry?"

"When I first met you, I saw you angry all the time. If

anyone mentioned your wife, you became outraged."

"That's because I don't want to think about her. I'm not angry with other people. I'm just mad. I've tried to get over that. I don't think I'm as bad as I was." He turned his head and looked at her. Am I? And when we first saw each other, I wasn't angry. I wanted you as much as you wanted me. I believe you remember that. You and I will come together at the right time."

Missy wasn't going to discuss what they wanted when they first met. "No, you're not as bad. I see you smile once in a while. And I've even heard you laugh."

"Oh, yeah, when did you hear me laugh?"

"When you swam in the river and Harold threw the football to you, it hit the rock and bounced back and hit Harold."

"Yeah, that was so funny. I feel like Harold is a part of my family. I don't have anyone since my mother died the same week my wife did."

"I'm sorry, that must have been so hard for you. No wonder you were always so angry."

"I wasn't angry. Maybe I was for a while. It didn't seem fair that I would lose the only two members of my family I had. So I might have felt sorry for myself. I just wanted to get away, so I got on my bike and left for a while."

"Four years is more than a while. I don't blame you. If I could drive a motorcycle, I would have left for a while too. But your friends thought you were a little destructive toward yourself. Hey, it's none of my business if you want a different woman every night. Plus, I guess as long as you took tests often to make sure you didn't have a disease, or two, you could have sex five times a night with different women."

Luke chuckled at that. "That's too much even for me. So why did you want to get away."

"When my grandma died, Polly moved in with me. I felt bad because her career was in full swing. I got involved with my P.E teacher, which was a nightmare. I was seventeen. Our neighbor was a biker. One day he heard me crying, so he took me on a ride on his bike. It was the most freeing experience I had ever had. I bought myself a motorcycle when I started making money."

"Oh yeah, what did you do with it?"

"I still have it. I've never driven it. It's in the same spot it was when I bought it. It's in Zane's garage. He wanted to show me how to drive it, but I chickened out," Missy chuckled. I always thought I was so brave. But I wasn't."

"You have always struck me as someone who is brave. You are an entrepreneur. You always let your friends in on all of your adventures. Heck, you've made me rich by letting me become an investor in your projects. That has to be scarier than hell, investing all that money for everyone. You help everyone you meet. Harold told me you said he was your little brother. And you've set up a college fund for him. Missy, you're a great human being."

"Thank you. I mean, I have extra money. Why not help someone who needs it. He will probably get a scholarship. He's exceptionally bright. But either way, the money is in his account. I love him like he is my little brother. He's very funny. Every time I'm around him, he makes me laugh. I'm thankful he's going to be alright." She took in a deep breath as if all was well with the world. "Thank you for coming with me," she said, turning her head to smile at him.

"You're welcome. You can sleep if you want to. You must be pretty tired with all that driving."

"Yeah, I am a little tired," she admitted as a yawn escaped her. Missy covered her mouth, shock written all over her face. Luke started laughing and the two of them were in hysterics for more than a minute. Missy could feel her stomach starting to hurt. "I can't continue laughing like this," she told him.

Luke looked at her, the urge to kiss her filled him but he thought better of it. The car was now void of laughter, the two of them feeling the tension pass between them.

"Get some rest," Luke said.

"Yeah, I'll do that," Missy replied as she rolled up her coat and used it as a pillow. When she woke up, they were pulling into a hamburger joint.

"Are you hungry?"

"Yes, I don't think I've eaten today. Where are we?"

"We're in Missoula. I thought we could get a room here."

"Okay, let's take our food with us." They both got hamburgers and milkshakes. Then they found a Marriott's and got two connecting rooms.

"Let's eat in my room. This looks good. I'm hungrier than I thought I was." They sat at the table in Missy's room and ate dinner. Luke got himself two hamburgers.

"Be sure you keep the door between our rooms opened. Just so I can hear if someone comes into your room," Luke said as he was leaving.

"Okay, goodnight." Missy threw all the empty hamburger stuff in the garbage. Then she opened her bag and took out something to sleep in. Missy walked to the bathroom. She turned on the shower, stripped out of her clothes, and stepped under the water. Missy craved for Luke to come in and join her in the shower. She started singing to get her mind off all the fantasies she knew would happen when Luke and she came together. She knew they would have wild passionate love together when they were both ready. She loved writing songs in her head while in the shower. Most of the time, she would make up songs in the shower. If she liked them she would write them down and tell one of her singer friends about them if she liked them.

LUKE COULD HEAR her singing as she showered. He had to get his mind off of a naked Missy Devlin. She was beautiful, inside and out. This was the most he'd talked to her since knowing her. Why is that? When they first met, he remembered that he told her they would be making wild, passionate love all night long. He chuckled. That was awful cocky of him. If he remembered right, she whispered her agreement to him. This was not the time to make love with her. This was the time to catch a killer who wanted her dead. He called Austin and told him what was going on. "You might want to keep an eye on Harold in case the guy comes back for him," he was saying.

"Missy hired the Band to guard Harold. Should I call anyone else to let them know where Missy is?"

"No, I don't think anyone knows where she is most of the time anyway. Doesn't she come and go whenever she wants. She's always alone unless she goes to her friend's house to visit them. Damn, she is always by herself. I've never really thought of that before. I guess because when I do see Missy, she's at someone's house. So that's like what, one day a week." Luke shook his head. "I wonder if she gets lonesome."

"I don't know. Probably. I guess, I naver thought about her living alone."

Luke didn't think he said that out loud until Austin answered him. "I'll talk to you later, Austin."

"Okay, keep your eyes peeled."

"Yep, always." Luke heard Missy's water go off and walked into his bathroom to take a cold shower. He knew no cold water was going to help this time. When he walked back into her room to make sure everything was locked up, the lights were out.

"Goodnight, Luke."

"Goodnight."

6

*A*s soon as he stepped into her darkroom, he knew she was gone. His heart fell to the pit of his stomach. Where the hell is she? He turned the lights on and looked around to see if she left a note. He didn't see anything. Luke started dressing and was heading out the door when her door opened. He knew she had gone jogging because she wore her workout clothes. Damn, she was hot. In the entire time he'd known her, he couldn't remember her dating anyone.

"Why the hell didn't you tell me you were going out? You scared the hell out of me."

"I did? I'm sorry, I'm not used to telling anyone that I'm going somewhere. I promise next time I'll leave a note."

"Thank you. You'll get used to this rule when you are with me. You don't go out jogging without me."

"Why is that a rule? I brought you some coffee," Missy said, looking at how damn handsome he was without his shirt on. *Stop looking at him.*

"Thank you. It's a rule because I'm trying to keep you safe."

"I told you I didn't need a bodyguard. Why don't you drink your coffee and I'll shower. Then we can leave."

"Fine," Luke walked back into his room and finished dressing. He had to get away from her before he pulled her to him and had his way with her. Damn, he didn't know if he could be with her and not take her to bed.

They were walking to their vehicle when Luke turned and looked at her. "How come I never see you with someone? Don't you date?"

"That's a personal question. But I will tell you, I don't date because I'm in love with someone."

Luke stopped walking, "What, why is he not with you right now? Why isn't he the one to run away with you? Why the hell isn't he guarding you?"

"He doesn't know I love him."

"How could he not know? Why haven't you told him?"

"Because I don't want to tell him. He's a stupid ass who has no idea I even exist."

"Believe me, I'm positive he knows you exist. He would have to be blind not to notice you. What are you wearing?"

"I'm wearing my leggings and a tank top. Why?" Missy shook her head and looked at Luke. Damn, he was blind. He didn't even know that one touch from him, and she was all his.

"Don't you have anything that will hide that sexy body of yours?"

"Ohhhh, you think my body is sexy?" Missy teased.

Luke couldn't believe he had said that aloud. He blushed. "Hell yes, I think your body is sexy. I'm not going to say anything else about your body."

Missy smiled.

Luke was jealous of a man he didn't even know. Missy probably loved one of those famous singers she hung out with all the time. He wondered why he never got to know her before now. Sure, he forced himself not to be near her because he knew he wanted her. There were so many people telling him to stay away from Missy. He didn't want to fight with them, but now he would tell them to go screw themselves. That guy she thought she loved didn't count because he was stupid. If he didn't know Missy loved him, then he didn't deserve her.

Missy knew Luke was thinking about what she said. She could almost feel his brain shifting through everything. "Why are you interested in my life?"

"Maybe because I've been warned so many damn times to stay away from you that I'm intrigued why they guard you the way they do"

"I don't know why. I'm always going by myself. They don't seem concerned about me when I'm traveling everywhere. I bet they haven't even noticed I'm gone."

"They know you're gone. I called Austin and told him where I was."

"You didn't tell him where we were going, did you?"

"No, but why don't you want them to know?"

"Because I like having a spot to myself. Harold knows I have a cabin in North Carolina. He just doesn't know where it is."

"I think that could be dangerous for you. What if you fell and broke a leg and couldn't get help. From now on, can you please let me know where you're going?"

Missy stared at Luke as he drove down the freeway. *He cares about me, doesn't he?* "I guess I could tell you. I never thought about myself getting hurt. There is a great place to run there. It's a hiking trail. I've only seen a few people on it. Oh, by the way, we should stop and get my car at the airport. It's full of dried food and can food. We can get some dried meat before we go up. The cabin is really high up. It reminds me of the old days I've seen in photos and on television. Once I came up here for an entire month, it was fantastic. I thought I should get home before Polly had a heart attack. When I got home, Riley wanted to know where the hell I'd been. She said I had to let her know if I was going to disappear. Everyone else has a family and kids, so it didn't bother anyone except Riley when I didn't show up for a month."

Luke reached over and took her hand. "It bothered me as well. I asked everyone if they knew where you were."

Missy took her hand back, shocked at this admission from him. "Oh, really. Tell me when that was."

"It was in the fall. You were gone the entire month of October."

"Yes, it was. How come you knew I was gone?"

Luke shrugged his shoulders, "I notice things like that about everyone. It's something I do. I always have."

"You notice when I'm not there. Why? I mean, I don't always live near where the Seals live."

"There doesn't have to be a reason. Sometimes my mind does something on its own. It's not like I'm keeping track of where you are. Anyway, why aren't you at Zane and Polly's more? They're your family."

"They have the kids, and it's their time to enjoy them. I used to stay there quite often. I love Taylor, and we still do a lot of things together. But Taylor was a teenager when Zane found out about him and he had a horrible life before that. They need time with him. He's in his second year of college this year. They go on vacation next week."

"Where are they going?"

"I don't know."

If Zane and Polly were sitting beside him, he would knock the crap out of both of them. Didn't they realize they were Missy's only family? They should include her in things that a family does.

"Do you know Piper?"

"Sure, I do. She is a genius with landscaping. Piper and I have some ventures together.

Piper isn't afraid to take chances. That's where I've learned so much. She taught me how to go with my feelings. She's the one who got me started making money. It's simple if you relax and don't stress over everything. You keep your eyes open and see what is popular with the teenagers. The teenagers are the ones who will make you money because when they like something, every teen on the planet wants it."

"So that's how you know about games?"

"Well, I actually play games. And Taylor and a few of his friends keep me informed on what's popular. For a bit of money, they have me on their caller I.D."

"Do you ever stop?"

"Yes. I stop when I'm with my friends and family. The only reason I work all the time is because I have so much time on my hands. You stay busy, so you don't understand what I mean."

"I understand what you are talking about. I stay busy because I have nothing to do when I'm off work. So I end up giving my vacation time to the guys who have a family."

"Here I was thinking you were a hard ass, but you're not."

"Yes, I am."

Missy laughed out loud. She thought that was so funny. When they went into another town for the night, they decided to eat at a restaurant. When Missy walked in, the men turned their heads. Not only was she beautiful, but she had the grace of a queen. She wore jeans with holes in them and a short white T-shirt with sandals.

Missy noticed the women stare at Luke when he walked into the restaurant. She looked at him and smiled to herself.

How could she not love him? She remembered he told her they were going to make love all night long. She would be ready if he still wanted to make love with her. Missy decided she would live a little and take some chances. What could happen? They would have fun. She would love him more, and he would go home. Okay, she was getting ahead of herself. Maybe she wouldn't make love with him. It would be too painful when she saw him with another woman.

7

The cabin was like something pictured on a Christmas card. There was one large room with the kitchen and family room. Two bedrooms, one at each end of the cabin. The view was out of this world. They sat on the front porch and watched the sun go down over the Blue Ridge Mountains. It was breathtaking. "How do you even leave this place?"

"That's why I stayed up here for a month. To me, these beautiful mountains are healing. I don't think of work or anything that's upsetting."

"What is upsetting for you?"

"Being hunted like an animal by a person who blames me for his parent's death."

"What are we going to do about Shawn?"

"I don't know. That's why I came up here. I thought maybe I could figure something out without him being around. Given he tried to kill Harold, I don't want to confront him. He never liked me. He tried to get me to go out with him a few times. I would never have gone out with him. Shawn always had that look about him. Kind of like he was a sneaky snake. He always had hate in his blood."

"I imagine he really became angry when you became involved with his father."

"I was never really involved with him. After my grandma died, I felt all alone. Polly moved in with me, but she was busy and away most of the time. My teacher was always wrapping his arms around me. He befriended me. He was always there for me. Now I know that's how he planned it. He would hunt for me after school, and we would stay in his office and talk. He kissed me a few times and one day, he took it further and further. Until we had sex. I didn't like it, so I told him I didn't want to be with him. He kidnapped me and brutally raped and beat me, for two weeks."

A gut-wrenching pain went through Luke. He clenched his jaw, almost biting his tongue when he did. "I'm sorry that happened to you. He deserved to die. I'm thinking his son follows in his father's footsteps."

"Yeah, I'm pretty sure he does. He was always angry at the world. Since he was in the second grade, he was a mean bully."

"How did you find this place? It's so far away from everywhere."

"A friend told me about it. She lives down the hill not too far. The first time I saw it was winter. It's beautiful in every season. But the house I have in Montana is my favorite."

"Why do you keep a house in Nashville and California?"

"Because I have friends in both places. But I've been thinking of selling all of my homes except this one and Montana. I mean, why should I have a house in California and one in Nashville. I don't need them." She had that urge to throw herself at him again all of a sudden. Missy stood up instantly, "I'll see you in the morning."

"Okay, I'll see you in the morning." Luke watched her walk away. He wondered what it was about Missy that made him want to take care of her. Since he'd known her, she has always taken care of herself. Now that he's seen this place, he didn't believe he had to worry about someone finding her here. He imagined he didn't have to stay here with her. But he decided he would anyway. He walked inside and locked the doors and windows. He laid in bed for hours thinking about Missy in the other bedroom.

A knock woke him up. He flew out of bed, forgetting he only had his boxers on. Luke opened the door, and Missy stood there. She backed up and raised her eyes to his face. He could tell she was embarrassed. Then she smiled.

"I'm going running. I'll be back in a couple of hours."

"Wait a minute, and I'll go with you." She nodded once and turned around. Luke pulled some shorts out of his bag and put some running shoes on and walked out of the room.

"Don't you want to wear a shirt?"

"No, will it bother you if I don't wear one?"

"No, not at all," she lied. Missy led the way.

They ran up the mountain on the trail. Luke was surprised how far Missy ran. They had gone a good ten miles before they got back to the cabin. Missy plopped down on one of the chairs on the porch. Luke sat on the other one. "When did you start running that many miles?"

"I've always run this far. I just didn't tell Riley. I didn't want her to feel I changed my miles for her. She would have felt bad."

Luke wanted to pull her to him and make love to her.

"The shower is cold, but it works. I'll take mine first."

"Okay." Luke was still sitting on the porch when he heard someone walking. He stood up when he saw a dog come running. The dog stopped when he saw Luke. He growled, and the hair on the back of his neck stood up.

"Sheriff, stop." A woman stepped into view. "Hello, who are you?"

"Luke Wilson. Who are you?"

"Kathy Reed. I'm a friend of Missy's. I thought I saw her running this morning from my porch."

"She's in the shower."

"Here I am. Hi, Kathy. Hey, Sheriff, come on, baby. Sheriff ran up the steps and jumped on Missy. She laughed and hugged him. "Thank you for keeping Sheriff for me. I was going to pick him up. You didn't have to walk all the way here."

"I know I didn't, but when I saw you and this guy running, nothing could keep me from coming here."

Missy laughed. She knew Kathy was gay, so she didn't have to worry about her flirting with Luke. She shook herself. Why would she have to worry? Luke wasn't hers. "This is Luke Wilson.

"I know, we already introduced ourselves. Kathy looked over at Luke and smiled. "So this is your…"

Missy didn't let her finish. "Luke, you can use the shower if you want."

"Great." He turned to Kathy, "It was nice meeting you."

"It was nice meeting you too."

Luke excused himself and walked inside. As soon as he left, Kathy grabbed Missy's arm and pulled her away from the porch. "Is that your Luke?"

"He's not my Luke."

"He's here with you, so he's something."

"He's here as a friend. He doesn't know I fell in love with him at first sight. My God, that sounds so stupid," Missy caught herself quickly. She covered her mouth, and Kathy chuckled waving her hand letting Missy know she should carry on. "If it hadn't happened to me, I would say that it's crazy. I do not want Luke to know about that," she waved a warning finger.

"I'm surprised he doesn't already know. I mean, you've told everyone, how could he not know?"

"Oh brother, do you think he knows?"

"No, or he would have done something by now. You did tell me he told you that the two of you were going to…"

"Stop. Don't say another word. Do you want something to drink?"

"Are we finished talking about him and sex?"

"Yes."

"Okay, I'll take a glass of water, then I have to go. My parents are coming to visit me."

"What? You haven't seen them in three years. I thought they disowned you?"

"They did, but they want to visit. Maybe they are ready to apologize for being so mean to me. I have to tell you something?"

"What?"

"I'm pregnant."

"You are. That's surprising." It was a good thing Missy couldn't see the look on her own face. It was a mixture of surprise mixed with confusion and a hint of disbelief.

"Well, I had sex with this guy. Sometimes I do that. So I must be bisexual. This guy is so cool. He has the greenest eyes. He is sweet, and I love his voice. He's from Louisiana. I thought if I had a child, I would want them to be like him. So I had sex with him."

"Does he know you're pregnant?"

"No, I haven't told him yet. I'm not sure I'm going to."

"I think that's wrong. If he's a good guy and you trust

him, then you should tell him. But hey, what do I know. What's his name?"

"Marc Breaux. I met him on the beach in California."

"Marc?" Missy took a deep breath, "I know Marc. And you are right. He is a great guy. I'm surprised he didn't take precautions. That doesn't sound like him."

Kathy felt excitement surge through her at the possibility they were really talking about the same Marc. "I told him I took precautions. Tell me about him."

"He is a Band of Navy Seals team member. He raised his little sister when their parents died. He would never turn his back on his child. You need to talk to him."

It was definitely the right guy. "I know. Wow, so you know Marc. Small world, right. I have to go."

"Good luck with your parents. Do they know you're pregnant?"

"No, I don't think I'm going to tell them. I'm not even sure what they want to say to me."

"Ring the bell if you need anything."

"I will. I'll be back before you leave."

"Come on, Sheriff, let's eat."

"I agree with you. Marc has a right to know if he's going to be a father. I won't say anything to him. Hopefully, she does," Luke said and he opened the door.

"Yeah, if she doesn't, then I will have to tell him. Are you hungry?"

"I'm starving."

Missy laughed. "Me too."

"So, Sheriff belongs to you?"

"Yes, I left her with Kathy the last time I was here. I got her a few months ago, but I wasn't going home right away, so Kathy kept her for me."

"You named your female dog Sheriff."

"Sure, some females are Sheriffs. In fact, it was a female Sheriff who gave her to me."

Luke laughed, "Are you pulling my leg?

"Nope," she crossed her heart, "cross my heart. I went to a party in Ashville and Ava, she's the Sheriff, was there. Her dogs didn't get along with Sheriff. I think they were jealous because she's so pretty. She reminded me of your dog, Rain, so I said I would love to take her. I had her in Nashville with me. She does not like the plane. I couldn't put her through that again. So Kathy kept her for me."

"So you were coming up here anyway?"

"Yes, I planned my visit for next week. I just came a week early because I heard about Shawn looking for me. If you get me some wood, I'll start the stove," she changed the subject.

"I'll start the stove. You can get the food out." He walked back in with an arm full of wood not long after. "What are we having?"

"Omelets. I have everything for them."

"Your solar panels work good up here?"

"Yes, I'm luckier than most because my cabin has an open space. So it gets lots of light. There is a family with little ones that come every summer. I let them use my fridge for milk. I also have a generator I can use for emergencies."

"How long have you had this cabin?"

"Six years. The person I bought it from, her great-grandfather built it almost two hundred years ago. It had been empty for like fifty years. I hired someone to restore it and put in some solar panels and lights when I got it. The well was already here. And someone had it put inside. I just updated it some."

"You have a beautiful home right in the middle of the Blue Ridge Mountains."

"Thank you. I enjoy being here. I've come here for Christmas for the last few years."

"Does your family come here?"

"No, just me."

"Do you always spend Christmas alone?"

"Since I got older, I do. I come up here. I don't mind. I enjoy coming here. I usually see my friend Kathy. Sometimes we have dinner together. I read a lot, and I stay busy. I also plan more cyber games."

"What about Kathy's family?"

"They haven't had anything to do with her since she told them she was gay. But she said they were coming to visit her today. I'm hoping they will be kind to her. She hasn't seen her parents in three years. Breakfast is ready."

"Wow, you know how to cook. This looks delicious."

"Thank you. My grandma taught me to cook before she got sick."

"How old were you when she got sick?"

"I was thirteen."

"Thirteen, and you took care of your grandma?"

"Someone had to. She didn't want strangers taking care of her. Polly hired a nurse to come there a few days a week, but grandma chased her off."

"How did you get your schooling done?"

"My principal knew Grandma, so she got together with my teachers, and they sent my schoolwork home with me a few days a week."

"Did Polly know about this?"

"I didn't tell Polly anything. She was busy getting her career started. Then when she became famous, she was busy having concerts. I didn't mind. I loved my grandma. I didn't know what to do when she died. I went into her room to wake her up, and she was dead. I ran next door and got our biker friend. He called Polly and the ambulance. They wouldn't take grandma until the coroner came out and checked her. God, it seemed to take forever. I swear I waited outside crying for hours. I felt like the only person I had in the world was gone. I missed her so much."

Luke had never heard Missy talk about her life before. He wanted to strangle Polly and her grandma, but she was already dead. So instead, he listened.

"I'm sorry. My God, you must think I'm a complainer. Please don't think bad of my family. I promise you I don't. Now, stop me if I talk anymore."

Luke smiled, "I like hearing you talk."

"Why?"

"Because it's refreshing. You have a beautiful voice."

Missy rolled her eyes, "Oh, brother, that's the silliest thing I've ever heard." That's when she heard the bells going off. She jumped up. "It's Kathy. Let's go."

They jumped into the truck and took off. Sheriff jumped into the back of the vehicle. When Luke and Missy pulled onto Kathy's property, A man tried to pull Kathy into a car. "What's going on here?" Luke demanded.

"They are trying to take me away." Kathy cried as Missy pulled her away from the man. Missy looked at Kathy and could see they had hit her.

"Why do you want her to leave, and why does she have marks on her?"

"She has to get the devil out of her. I found someone to help us. He says the only way for her to be normal again is for us to take her to him." Missy turned around and watched the woman walk out of the house. She had a gun in her hand. "If she doesn't come with us I'll kill her right here. We have to get the devil out of her."

Luke kicked the gun out of the woman's hand and turned to see Kathy's father with a knife in his hand. "Listen to the two of you. This is your daughter, and some guy told you to kill her. What the hell is the matter with both of you? Missy, call the police. They need to be locked up for this."

LUKE

"I never want to see either of you again! You're not my parents! I disown both of you! Stay the hell away from me! Get out of here before I have you arrested."

Missy had her arms around her friend. "Is this the woman you have in your bed?" Kathy's father shouted. "I'll kill her." He ran at Missy with his knife up over his head. A fist went past Missy's head, and the man fell to the ground.

"Call the police, or I'm going to kill him. Sit on the ground next to your husband. I can't believe you two would try to kill your daughter. You're lucky your knife didn't touch one hair on Missy's head. I would have killed both of you if it had."

Missy hugged Kathy. I'm sorry you have them for your parents. Have they always been like this?"

"No, they joined a church about five years ago. They started changing not long after that. That's why I moved here. They were always pressuring me to join. They even had their pastor come to my house to try and pressure me. That guy scared me. The way he stared at me. I believe it's a cult. When I told my parents what I thought, they freaked out. I had hoped they went back to normal when I heard they were coming here. When I told them I was gay, that was the last I've heard from them, until now."

"Katherine needs to be beaten until the devil comes out of her body. She is a lesbian. If we don't remove him from her body, then we have to kill her. The pastor said it was the only way to get the devil out."

The police showed up with their sirens blaring.

"I want that man arrested. He hit me and knocked me out," Kathy's father said.

Luke looked at the guy, "He's lucky I didn't kill him. He charged Missy with a knife."

The police looked over at Missy, "How's Sheriff doing?"

45

"She's good. Kathy watched her for a few weeks. Maybe I should leave Sheriff with you," Missy said, looking at Kathy.

"No, I'm going to go away for a while. I will be back to testify against my parents. I'm pregnant, and they tried to kill my baby and me."

"Did they know that you are pregnant?"

"Yes, I told them I was pregnant. Hoping it would help my parents except me more. But all it did was to make them go crazier. They need to be locked up, or I'm afraid they'll kill my baby and me. They belong to a cult, and the so-called pastor told them to kill me. All because I'm gay."

8

They had been at the cabin for over a week. As Luke and Missy ran that morning, Missy looked over at Luke. "I have to run to town. I'm sure I'll be fine if you want to leave. I believe I'm safe. I don't think Shawn knows where I am."

"Do you want me to leave?"

"No, but I know you have a life. I'm sure you have more things to do than babysit me."

"I like being here. I don't have any place to go. I'll run you into town."

"Okay. We could drive around, and I can show you some fantastic views around here."

"That sounds like fun. Maybe we'll have dinner in town."

"I know a place that serves crabs, and they are delicious."

"Sounds good to me. I love crab meat." Luke knew he should get the hell away from Missy. He was starting to have strong feelings for her. He had promised himself that would never happen again. He actually never talked to a woman as much as he has spoken to Missy. Susan's face flashed in his mind, and he frowned. He didn't want to think of her today.

Every time he thought of his wife, he became angry. It wasn't fair that she was killed, and he lived. Luke knew he should have picked her up and pressured her to leave with him. But that didn't happen, and he had to live with her death.

"What's wrong?"

He shook his head. "Nothing's wrong."

"Are you sure? You don't look very happy."

"Do people have to be happy all the time? I know you like people to be happy all the time, but believe me when I tell you that's not realistic. Most people are miserable. You don't run into someone who's happy all the time. Except maybe you."

"Are you finished?"

Luke ran his fingers through his hair and shrugged his shoulders. "I'm sorry. I thought all this misery was behind me, but I guess it's not. I think you're right. I better get back to my job. We can get that crab another time?"

"Sure. I can still run you into town."

"That's okay. I have a jeep in the shed."

"You do?"

"Yeah." Missy walked to the kitchen and got the keys. "Come on, Sheriff. Can you lock the cabin up when you leave?"

"Sure I can." *What the hell is wrong with me. Why am I doing this to Missy? It's because I like being with her way too much. I could never put her ahead of my wife. I'm a fucking idiot.* Luke sat in the chair on the porch. He didn't even know his wife. She was someone he knew three days when they married. She was so sexy, and sex with her was great. That's why he asked her to marry him. No, she asked him to marry her. *But that's not why I married her. I loved Susan. We were married for three years. Yes,* a little voice in his head said. *But you were only together for a total of six months.*

Six months. Why were we together so little time? Luke

thought back over his life with Susan and that last day with her. When Luke talked to her lieutenant, she said Susan had her papers to leave. But when he confronted Susan, she said she had to stay. Why was she staying instead of going with her husband? Every time they were around each other, they argued.

Luke sat there on the front porch and went over his marriage with Susan. It was good the first few months, but after that, it wasn't so great. *Why have I mourned her if it wasn't so great? Guilt, I feel guilty for her not leaving with me. Instead, she stayed and died. She would be alive if she listened to me. Why did she want to stay there instead of going with her husband? Things never added up, but every time my thoughts went this way, I would stop thinking about it. Now I want to know.*

He called Dallas. "Hey, Dallas, do you think I could stop by and talk to you."

"Sure."

"Where are you?"

"I'm in Nashville. But I'll be at Austin's in a few days."

"Great, I'll see you in a few days." Luke got his things and threw them in his truck. It was time all of his doubts were brought into the open.

MISSY KNEW Luke was feeling guilty about having a good time with her. She knew that look. Every time his thoughts went to Susan, he shut down. *I don't have time to wait around for him anymore. He can live in his head with thoughts of his cheating wife. I'm over it. I've wasted a long time with my heart breaking over Luke Wilson. I really thought things were going good for us. I wanted him to make love to me. I thought he wanted that as well.*

Missy didn't bother putting her wig back on. She stopped

at Verizon and got a new phone. That was stupid of me to break my phone and throw it away. She also got an I pad so she could take care of her business. She didn't bring her computer. She went grocery shopping and then she called Harold.

"How are you?"

"I'm going home today. Theodore is going to go by your house and make sure it's all picked up."

"He doesn't have to do that. I'm so glad you feel better. I want you to kick back and let your family take care of you."

"My mom is working with Julia now. Julia was at the hospital visiting me when my mom came in. She asked Julia about her shop, and then they were talking about pies, and I told Julia what a great pie maker my mom is, and she hired her. Julia told her she could bring my little brother and sisters to the shop when they get out of school. It was perfect. My mom cried."

"I'm so happy for her. Julia must be so delighted that she has someone to help her. Besides Austin. I bet he's happy as well."

"Austin is still going to make her some pies, one day a week. How are you? Is Luke still with you?"

"No, he left today. He'll be visiting you soon. You take care of yourself, Harold. I'll see you when I get back home. I'll call you in a couple of days."

"Okay, bye Missy. I'll see you when you get home. Be careful."

"Yes, I'll be careful. Don't worry about me; I'll be fine."

Missy decided to make a day of it. She went and did some shopping, then she stopped and had crab meat for her dinner. It was good, but she was sure it would have been better if Luke was there with her. *No more feeling sorry for yourself.* She got up, climbed into her jeep, and went home.

9

Three weeks later, Luke was still angry that he hadn't seen the real Susan. Of course, they were hardly ever together. He had no idea she was dating Dallas when he ran away with her and eloped. Dallas actually thanked him because he said he was going to propose to her. Luke closed his eyes to everything about Susan. What an idiot he was. The only thing he thought about was how much he thought he loved her. Now he didn't even know if he loved her anymore.

When Dallas told him that she died with her lover, who was also married, Luke was pissed. He'd talked to Dallas and a few others, then he let his mind remember the not-so-good times he had with Susan. He wanted to kick himself for being so stupid. She had been cheating on him a couple of months after they married. He wished he had known about her infidelity back then. He would have divorced her. It hurt that she did that, but not as much as he thought it would. He was angrier at himself for acting like an idiot when she died. Maybe most of his sorrow was because he missed his mom, and he thought it all was for Susan.

Luke thought of Missy. He could have been with Missy all this time. He knew when they came together, it would be different than anything he's ever experienced before. *When she gets back home, we are going to have a long talk about us.* He almost went back to her cabin. But decided to wait and see how she acted toward him when she came home. He actually thought she would be home by now. He was still on the hunt for Shawn. He was wanted for running Harold down with his vehicle and leaving him for dead. His phone rang, and he answered.

"Hi, Luke."

"Hey Harold, how are you doing?"

"I was wondering if you talked to Missy."

"No, I haven't talked to her. When was the last time you heard from her?"

"I can't get a hold of her. She told me she would call me every two days, but I haven't heard from her in four days. Missy always does what she says she's going to do."

"Have you asked anyone else if they've talked to her?"

"No, I only asked you. I'll check with the others. She might be at Zane's house."

"No, they are in Ireland on vacation." *Another vacation without Missy.* "Okay, Harold, I'll call around."

"Call me back, please."

"I will." Luke hung up and called everyone. He even called Zane.

"We are in Ireland on vacation."

"I thought maybe Missy went on vacation with her family."

"No, why would you think that?"

"Because you're her family. Doesn't she usually go with you and Polly on vacations? Since you are the only family, she has."

"No, she doesn't."

"Who does she take vacations with?"

"I don't know. She used to go with us before we had the kids. I don't know why she stopped."

"Maybe you stopped asking her."

"I don't think we would have done that. I'm sure we asked Missy. We wouldn't just leave her out. She has always been a part of our lives."

"Oh, like Christmas every year when familes get together."

"What? Fuck. I'll see you in a couple of days. Why are you hunting for Missy?"

Luke explained everything to Zane. "I won't be here. I'm going to Missy's cabin in North Carolina."

"Missy has a cabin in North Carolina? Why didn't I know she had a cabin there?"

"I don't know why you didn't know. But yes, and she has Christmas there by herself every fucking year. You're a fucking ass hole," Luke said as he hung up on Zane. He was so angry, not only at himself for being so stupid. He was angry because Zane and Polly forgot they had another family member out there all alone.

He called Harold back and told him he was going to find Missy."

"If my leg wasn't broken, I would go with you."

"I know you would. Call me if you hear anything."

"I will."

Luke packed a bag and called Kane to fly him to North Carolina.

"Why do you think Missy is missing?"

"She told Harold she would call him every two days. I think she did that because she wasn't quite sure that Shawn wouldn't come after her. He may have found out where she is. I hope to hell he hasn't found her."

"I'll go with you to find her."

"No, you take me, and if I need help, I'll call you."

"I don't like this. Now I'm worried about Missy. It's been a while since I last saw her. When did she leave?"

"She's been gone for over a month. Maybe her phone needs charging. She has solar, so she can get electricity when she needs it. If there is good weather."

∽

MISSY RAN another five miles before she allowed herself a break. *How did he find me? I was too sloppy. I can't believe I let myself stop wearing a wig. I forgot to be careful. I know why I did, because Luke was with me, and I felt safe. Now I'm running for my life.*

Her only hope was that she could outrun Shawn. Missy was used to running in these hills. She has run every day since she got here. She had to find a spot to rest. She has been on the run for two days. Missy didn't dare run in the dark. It was too dangerous. She was so scared. Missy couldn't fight like her friends. Sure, Julia taught her some moves to save herself, but she didn't think she could really do it. She should have brought Sheriff with her instead of putting him in a kennel. He would take care of Shawn for her. But she was going to get the car she bought and she didn't want to take Sheriff. Now he's in a kennel, instead of the two of them driving home as she planned. She couldn't even call the kennel and tell them where she was because she dropped her phone when Shawn showed up, and she was scared.

What was that? I can hear something. Missy hid behind a large tree. *Missy, you have to look and see what is going on. You can't stay behind the tree forever. Oh God, Oh God, Missy, just do it.* She peeked to see if she could see anything. She turned her head to the left, and a massive bear was watching her. She actually felt relieved that it wasn't Shawn. *Maybe the bear will*

LUKE

go away. She shrugged her shoulders and ran up the mountain. She was surprised at how far up she had gone. She didn't have time to notice the beautiful trees or the view. She had to make sure Shawn didn't find her. She could smell the forest all around her. It calmed her a little.

While she ran, she would turn her head to see if the bear followed her. She didn't see any sign of the bear. At least that was one thing she didn't have to worry about. She lost her phone somewhere outside her cabin, so she wasn't able to call anyone. She worried if Kathy would come back. She didn't want this crazy bastard anywhere around a pregnant Kathy.

Missy knew she was lucky that she spotted Shawn in her cabin before he saw her. She had been on her run when she returned home, she spotted the vehicle in her driveway. Her heart soared, thinking Luke had come back. But she saw Shawn through the large front window, and she panicked. He heard her cry out, and when she stumbled away from her cabin, she fell down and dropped her phone. How she got so far ahead of him, she didn't know. But she had more strength than she knew she had.

It had turned dark. She would find an easy maple tree to climb, and then she would make a spot to sleep. Even if it was only an hour at least, she had an hour of sleep. She used the pack that she still had on her from her run. Thank goodness she still had water in it. And those protein bars Luke threw in when he was here. She took a swallow of water and a bite of her protein bar. That was all. She didn't know how long she would be here in these mountains.

Missy looked around her. The dogwood trees were beautiful. She hadn't been this high up before, and she didn't have time to admire it right now.She did wonder if maybe there was a cabin up here. But then again if she found it then Shawn would find it as well. Sometimes the locals would come up here and make moonshine. She wished she would come across some of those people. She felt her face and realized she had been crying. *What the hell is wrong with me? I don't have time to cry.* She wiped her tears on her shoulder.

Missy knew she needed to take a break. She hoped Shawn was out of shape, and he never caught up with her.

～

"Why did you have to tell Julia? You knew she would want to come with us."

"I had to tell her where I was going. She's my wife. She had me spilling my guts before I knew what was happening."

"Calm down, Luke. Are you forgetting who I am? Hell, if Missy is missing, I can help find her. Do you know how many people I've found? A hell of a lot more than you. So shut the fuck up, Luke. I have to think."

Luke shook his head, "Just don't get in my way."

"You, don't get in my way."

"Would you two shut up? How much further up is her cabin?" Kane said, looking at both of them.

"Not far." When Luke went around the last bend in the road, he knew she wasn't there. The cabin's door was opened, and there wasn't a fire going. "She's not here, and her door is opened. At this time in the morning, she runs, but something has happened here." He jumped out of the truck and walked through the cabin. He felt the stove and knew it'd been a few days since she had a fire burning in her stove.

Luke walked around the cabin. He looked down when something caught his eye. Her phone lay in the dirt. He went inside and got the key, and opened the shed. Her jeep was in there. That's when he saw the little car parked behind the shed. He wrenched the door open, he knew whose name he would see on the paper before opening the glove compartment. There on the rental lease was Shawn's name. Luke shouted. He was so angry. He ran inside and rang the bell. Maybe Missy would hear it and know he was here.

"What's the bell for?" Julia asked.

"When someone needs help, they ring the bell. Maybe we'll run into more people who will get the word out. Let's go." They got their backpacks and took off. "I hope you two can keep up with me."

"If we can't, then you keep going. We'll catch up later. Are you going to take the bell?"

"Yes, I'm going to keep ringing it so Missy can hear it."

"I hope she's able to hear it. We don't even know which way to go."

"She'll run up the mountain. Missy will stay off the trails. She can run for hours. Keep your ears and eyes open, we might come across this bastard who is trying to kill Missy."

Kane and Julia kept up with Luke for two hours, and then they decided to take a different trail. They could hear the bell ringing. It was kind of surreal to listen to the bell ring so clear, knowing it had to be far away. "Do you think she can hear the bell?"

"I pray she can hear it. Maybe if she can hear it, she'll know we're here hunting for her."

"Yes, I pray she's alright," Julia's voice cracked. She couldn't help it. Missy was her best friend. She should have called her. She didn't know that Missy was running from a crazy bastard. One who wanted her dead. "Why the hell wasn't I told about this fucking Shawn?"

Missy thought she was hearing things. She could barely hear the bell. But she knew that's what it was. It was her bell. Someone has it. Who would be ringing it? She kept running.

It might be a trick, she couldn't give in and go back down to check on it. She hoped it was someone genuine looking for her.

~

"What the hell is that noise. I must be hearing things. Damn, how far can she run? I can't believe she's still going up. I need some water and something to eat. How is she getting by without food and water? I'm going to beat her to death after I rape her a few times. I'm going to see what my old man was so obsessed with." Shawn was speaking to himself aloud like the maniac that he was. "Missy, can you hear me?" he called out in the woods. "I'm coming for you. When I catch you, I'm going to hurt you. I'm going to kill you, but first, I will hurt you. You have to slow down soon. And when you do, you're all mine."

"There goes that damn bell again. Where is it coming from? Damn, it's getting dark. I wonder if I can eat these berries. They look good. I'm sure if animals can eat them, then so can I." He picked a handful and shoved them in his mouth. They were a bit bitter tasting, but he didn't mind. He was too hungry to worry about the taste. He would give anything for some water. He finished the two bottles he had that morning. Maybe he would find a stream.

"Missy, you are going to be so surprised when I take you. I'm sure I'm much better than my father was. I'll have you yelling for more." He started laughing as he stuffed his pockets full of berries.

~

Luke found a water bottle on the ground and knew it wasn't Missy's. She wouldn't have thrown it down. Thinking about

LUKE

the guy being right behind Missy had him running harder. So he knew for sure the guy was chasing her. She must be so scared. Luke pushed himself. The sun was going down, he decided to keep going. He was pretty sure Missy would stop when the sun went down. Luke put on night goggles and kept going. He searched through the night but couldn't find her. He couldn't bear losing her. When the sun came up, he rang the bell again, hoping Missy heard it. The trail was easy to follow now.

He came upon some berries. Someone had picked them. He knew it wasn't Missy. She's the one who told him they were poisonous. Luke thought that would be good if Shawn ate some poison berries. It would for sure slow him down. Luke took out a protein bar and took a bite. Then he took a drink of water. *How do I even know she went this way?*

He kept walking, then he realized Missy had no doubt turned around. She wouldn't keep going up. If she heard the bell, she would know he was here. Plus, she would be trying to lose the guy who was after her. She would cut across and head back down to her cabin. So he walked left and hoped he would run into her soon. He rang the bell and hoped she heard it. That's when he heard the shot of a rifle pierce the air. He took off running.

Luke's heart slammed into his chest. He knew what he was going to find. He almost ran over her. She was covered in blood. Luke bent and picked her up.

"Shawn found me," she said before she blacked out.

"Stay awake, Sugar. Don't leave me."

"Get away from her." The guy was vomiting all over himself. His hand was shaking as he tried to hold the rifle straight.

"You lost Shawn. Put the gun down. It was your father who beat and raped Missy when she was a child. She has no blame for your parent's death. It was all on your bastard father. I'm going to tell you one more time to put the gun down, or I'm going to blow your fucking head off. Those berries you ate were poison."

"Get away from her!" Shawn shouted. He looked like something out of a horror movie.

Luke reached for his gun, he heard a gun fired, and Shawn fell to the ground. He turned his head as Julia put her weapon away. She ran to where Luke held Missy in his arms.

"Is she dead?" Julia cried.

Luke was busy trying to find where the bullet hit Missy. "I don't know. Wait, I can feel a pulse. I can barely feel it. But it's a pulse. That's all that counts. There it is. The bullet went into her side. We have to get her to a hospital. He turned around when Kane and three mountain men came through the trees on four-wheelers.

"Luke, this man is a doctor," Kane said, trying to take Missy from him. "Let him check her wound."

Luke stepped back as the doctor checked Missy's wound. "The bullet is still in there. A helicopter will meet us in the clearing."

"I'll hold Missy on the back of your four-wheeler."

"What about that guy there?" another man asked.

"He's dead," Julia spat angrily.

"I'll have someone bring him out. The bastard deserved to die," the doctor said.

"Yes, he did," Julia said, wiping a tear away.

10

Polly paced the hospital hallways. She wasn't alone. Every one of Missy's friends was there. Missy had been in the hospital for three days, now she was in surgery again. Because they saw something else, Luke had gotten into three fights since he got to the hospital. When the doctor said he didn't know if she would live, Luke roared like a man in pain. He didn't know why. He didn't care why, Zane stepped up to him, and Luke let him have it right in that pretty face of his. Polly wouldn't stop crying. So Luke walked away. The following person was Storm because he needed to hit someone.

This morning when the doctor said it didn't look good, Missy was burning up with fever. He hit the doctor. The cops came, the doctor didn't press charges, so he wasn't arrested. When he heard a voice asking for him, he turned, and his old friend Kash stood there.

"Kash, thank God you're here. Did you bring him?"

"Hello, Kash."

Kash turned around in time to see the fist flying straight

at his face. He ducked in time, and it hit Luke who growled as he looked around.

"Stop it right now. Zane, what the hell are you doing?" Polly demanded.

"I owe him. The last time I saw him, he sucker-punched me."

"How was I to know you were going to turn your back on me?"

"I was drunk. I didn't even know I turned my back on you."

"Shut up. Where is he?" Luke asked Kash.

"He is with Missy. I'm going to tell you I almost didn't bring him. He lives on an island by himself. He drinks homemade whiskey. He shot at me because he said he recognized me. He was so drunk. I got him to sober up enough to listen to me. Now, tell me who this woman is?"

"She's my friend. I told you what happened to her."

"So, who did you bring to look at her?" Rowan asked from behind.

"Damn, are all of you here?"

"Yeah, we run a business together. The Band of Navy Seals. So, who did you bring?"

"Angel."

"Angel, why the hell did you bring that crazy bastard?" Rowan asked, frowning at Luke.

"Because he's the best surgeon there is. And we all know it. We've seen him in action too many times. In the middle of a war, he's operated on men and women and saved their lives. He has saved more lives than any other doctor. I'm not going to watch Missy die. Angel Davis can do miracles. That is why he's here. And I want to remind you he's my friend. So if you think to say anything else about him, I wouldn't if I was you."

They stood near the surgery doors and could hear

shouting and swearing coming from the other side of the operating room door. Luke watched as a nurse came out with a smile on her face. She held her heart and mouthed, '*I love him.*'

Zane smirked. "I see Angel hasn't changed much since the last time we saw him. Women are still swooning at his feet. "

Luke shook his head, frowning. Damn, he was tired. "Who cares a fuck what kind of person he is. He'll save Missy. That's all that matters."

"You're right. That's all that matters. Let's go to the waiting room. It's going to be a while before the doctor comes out. So Kash, what have you been doing with yourself since we last saw you."

"Oh, I've kept myself busy. I've kept in touch with all of the Army Rangers in my squad. We run missions rescuing American's left behind in other countries and our affiliates who need us to save them. People who have helped us when we were in their country and who were promised a better life."

"I've heard good things about you guys. You have been busy. I'm glad to know the Special Forces are still fighting for us after they leave the service. "

"Thank you. We tried getting Angel to join us, but he refuses."

"What do I refuse?" Everyone in the waiting room looked at the doorway.

"How is Missy?" Luke asked, jumping up.

"She's going to be okay. There was one little tear inside her stomach lining that the good doctor missed. It got infected. It's all sewn up, and the infection should go away. If I hadn't seen before what a rifle could do to a body, I would have missed it too. The bullet will explode and go in all different ways. She is very fit, not an ounce of fat. She is all muscle. I gotta say she's one hot babe. Who does she belong to?"

"Angel, this is Polly. She's Missy's aunt."

Angel had a massive grin on his face, "Sugar, I love your songs. So you married Zane. He's a good guy. Your niece is going to be fine. She'll have to take it easy for a few weeks, but she should be as good as new in no time. Now tell me, why did someone shoot her with a rifle?"

Polly wiped her eyes. "A crazy bastard. This can go no further than this room. I don't want Missy's past brought up. It was hard for her to go through that horrible gossip. It was a nightmare for her."

"Yeah, I saw the scars on her back, so I figured she must have gone through hell. Luke, you can go see her. You look like crap man. You need to get some sleep and take a shower. How long has it been since you slept? Speaking of sleep, I'm going to get some shut-eye. I'll see you all later."

"Where are you going to sleep?"

"I'll find myself an empty room."

LUKE WAS SLEEPING on the chair next to her bed when Missy opened her eyes. Polly smiled at her, she was standing next to her bed, brushing her hair with her fingers. "How do you feel, honey?"

"Thankful I'm alive. I'm so thirsty. Could I get a drink of water?" She looked over at Luke. "Why is he sleeping in here?"

Polly shrugged her shoulders. "I don't ask him questions anymore. He's decked at least three men I know of, and one of them was Zane. He was terrified you were going to die. I'm going to go get the nurse."

"Okay." When Missy raised her eyes to Luke, their gazes met. She smiled.

"Hey, how do you feel?"

"I feel lucky I'm alive."

Luke reached for her hand and held it between his. "I'm sorry I wasn't with you."

"You didn't have to be with me. What happened to Shawn?"

"Julia shot him. He ate those poison berries you showed me."

Missy smiled and sighed with relief. "I'm glad I don't have to worry about him anymore. Are you tired?"

"A little."

"Come over here. You can rest next to me."

Luke reached the bed in one step. He laid next to her, and she went back to sleep. He kissed her forehead and closed his eyes.

When Polly walked in, they were both sleeping. She smiled. Missy picked the right man to fall in love with after all. She wasn't sure if Luke realized how lucky he was to have Missy love him. It might take some convincing for him to say he loved her, but Polly knew he did. He proved it the minute they got here.

11

"Hi, you look like you are doing pretty damn good, you must have a hell of a doctor."

Missy smiled. Her doctor Angel Davis was handsome, and the nurses loved him. His hair was in his eyes again. He couldn't be older than his mid-thirties. His eyes were dark green with long black lashes.

"I think he is. He's handsome too. So, do I get to go home today?"

"Yes. Where are you going? Polly says you're going home with her. I don't think Luke is going to let that happen. He says you're going to your house, and he's going to take care of you for a few weeks. Which one are you going to choose?"

"I choose Luke."

"That's what I thought. I'll tell him what you said. Ash is going to fly you home. I'll be seeing you around Missy Devlin. It was an honor to meet you."

"Thank you for saving my life. Doctor Angel, you should come to my house. There is excellent fishing right out my front door."

"I'll take you up on that one day, Missy. He bent his head

and kissed her. If you weren't in love with Luke, I would give him a run for his money. You'll have to visit my island sometime."

"You can count on it. Bye Angel."

"Bye, darling."

Missy smiled, watching him go out the door. She grabbed her things and followed him out. She walked out the front door and caught a Taxi. And had him drive her to her cabin. Smiling, she thought about how surprised they would all be when they found out she was already gone.

"WHERE DID SHE GO?" Polly asked. Looking around at the empty room, she saw the note on the pillow. Listen to this. *"Polly and Zane, thank you for everything you do for me. I'm going home. I will see you at Christmas as we planned. I love you and Zane and the kids. Tell Taylor he can stop worrying about me. I'm going to be fine. Tell Luke I'm at the cabin. He*

might have to do some grocery shopping before he comes up. I love you, Missy.'"

"I'll see you two around. I have some groceries to buy." Luke smiled as he walked out the door.

Polly smiled, "Let's go home to our kids. Maybe everything will work out for Missy. I hope so. She deserves to have someone love her, the same way you love me."

"I do love you, sweetheart. Let's call Taylor and tell him we're on our way."

LUKE WAS sure he bought too much food. He didn't care. He purchased a strawberry cake and realized it goes in a fridge. *Oh well, we'll eat it first. I'm sure Missy is ready for some good food.* His mind went to his wife, Susan, he wished he could stop thinking of her, but she always crept in when he least expected. Their entire marriage was a lie. What was strange was that he didn't care that much anymore about the cheating. *Does that mean I didn't love her as much as I thought I did? I know that what I feel for Missy is a billion times stronger than what I felt for Susan. I don't know what I feel for her. I will never marry again. I will have to be careful, so Missy doesn't think I love her. I care for her because we are such good friends. I want her because she's so damn hot, and I want to be with her. But I will never fall in love with anyone again. It's not worth the pain. I'll talk to Missy about it.*

He parked the truck and grabbed a couple of bags. He didn't see Missy. The door had been left open. Only the screen was shut. He turned the handle and walked in. He put the bags down and went and got the rest of the food. Then he went hunting for her. She was sleeping in her bed, all curled up. Luke put the food away and started cooking hamburgers on the grill outside. He was eating a piece of the strawberry cake when he looked up and saw Missy watching him. She was wearing one of his T-shirts and sweats, she looked beautiful. He was instantly hard. Luke was glad he held his plate in his lap. He remembered loaning her that T-shirt when she rode on his bike when they first met. She kept his T-shirt to sleep in. What does that mean?

"I'm eating the cake for a reason. It needs to be in a fridge, so I have to eat it before it ruins. We have hamburgers for dinner."

"I have a small fridge we can put the cake in. But first, I want a slice. I'll eat my hamburger next. The cake looks delicious. What kind is it?"

"Strawberry. It is delicious. Let me get you some. How are you feeling?"

"I'm just tired. I love strawberry cake. I'll get it. Stay where you are. You should have woken me. I'm glad you were able to come here. I thought I could rest here for a while before I went home. I feel so weak. I'm sure I'll feel better soon. I didn't know if I would be scared or not. But I think I should be okay. You don't have to stay with me. Maybe just tonight."

"Do you want to tell me about what happened?"

"Let me get my cake first. Missy took a bite and got some on her lip. She licked it off. Strawberry cake is my favorite."

"Mine too," Luke whispered. He watched her tongue come out and lick her lips again. Damn, she needed to stop that. Luke shook himself so he would stop staring.

She looked at him and took a deep breath. Her chin wobbled, and a tear slipped down her cheek. "I'm sorry for being such a baby. I wish I was as strong as Julia and the others. I swear I was never so scared as when I looked in my window and saw Shawn in here. I had been out on my run when I got home I saw him. I turned around and took off, running back the way I came from. I dropped my phone when I heard him call my name. I was terrified. My heart was beating so hard I thought I would have a heart attack. I had just returned from running ten miles. He must have thought I would be easy to catch, or I'm sure he would have shot me in the back. But I pushed myself, and I got away from him. At one time, I came face to face with a Grizzly Bear. When I realized I was more scared of Shawn than I was the bear, I became more frightened."

Luke walked over to her, he picked her up, and sat down with her tucked comfortably on his lap. He's gone, so you don't have to be scared anymore. I'm here now. I'll stay for as long as you need me."

"That's not fair to you."

"Missy, I want to stay here. I want to help you. I feel bad because I wasn't here with you when he found you."

"Oh, brother," she rolled her eyes, "don't start that. You

are not responsible for me. Why in the world would you feel guilty?"

"Because I left."

"Of course, you did. You weren't supposed to stay indefinitely with me. I'm not your responsibility. I'm glad you are here now. As soon as I feel better, I'll go back to Montana. I've called all my friends and told them I'll be home when I'm feeling better. Do you have to go back to work?"

Luke smiled, "No, I don't have to. I'm going to stay with you and take you home when you are ready to go."

"Thank you. Did someone take Sheriff home?"

"Yes, she went on the plane with Kane and Julia. I'm sure she didn't like it." Luke was talking to her when he realized she was sleeping. "You rest, sweetheart," he whispered, "I'm not going anywhere."

12

*L*uke knew she would be the death of him if she kept wearing those short shorts of hers while she was cleaning. They were leaving for Montana, and Missy made sure the cabin was clean before she locked up. Every time she moved, he wanted to pull her up against him. She didn't try to make herself look beautiful. She was a natural beauty. She didn't wear make-up, and she didn't spend hours on her hair. He didn't want to compare her with other women, but he couldn't help it. She was stunning.

No other woman could compare with her. Luke shook his head as he laughed at his thoughts. She stayed busy all the time. If she rested, then she read a book. He spent his time cleaning up outside, picking up broken pieces of limbs. He was glad the police had already moved Shawn's rental car. He went through her shed and straightened it out. He hoarded every minute he could get in with Missy because he knew it wouldn't be long before they were back in Montana, and she would be at her house and he at his. He wanted to ask her out when they got home, but he was afraid she would think he wanted a permanent relationship with her.

"Luke, I'm all packed up. I'm ready if you are."

"Yes, I'm ready also. Are you ready to get back home?"

"Yeah, I guess I am."

"What do you mean you guess you are?"

"I hate leaving here. I enjoy the coziness. It's so comfortable with the fire going. I love this place. I'm going to start staying here more often."

"I agree, it's a great place to be. Plus, when you meet people on the trail, they are nice, but they stay to themselves."

"Exactly."

They climbed into Luke's truck and drove home. They had already sold Missy's used car that she had left at the airport. The drive was nice. They talked about everything under the sun, except Susan. Missy didn't mention her, and neither did Luke. When they stopped for the night, they each had a separate room with no connecting door. He took her home and unloaded her things.

"You can put everything right there. I'm going to wash it all. Thank you for everything. I'm going to miss you."

"I'm only a few miles down the road."

Missy giggled, "I know. I'll see you around. *Don't be a stranger*, as my grandma used to say. I'm going to walk down and get Sheriff at Julia's."

Luke took her hands and pulled her into his arms. "Call me for anything, and I'll be here."

"I know."

"Bye," he kissed her forehead and stepped back.

Missy watched as he drove away. She wiped the tear that fell, *Damn, I love him more than I thought I did.*

"How are you? I'm so glad you're home. Tell me about you and Luke?"

"There is nothing to tell except I love him more than I imagined I did. He was so sweet, and he helped me so much. He didn't even try to kiss me. There I was, ready for him to throw me on the bed and do whatever he wanted to do with me. I wanted him to make wild passionate love with me. I wanted hot, sweaty sex, but he didn't even touch me in that way. All I got was a kiss on the forehead when he dropped me off two days ago."

Julia laughed. "Do you miss him?"

Missy sighed, "Yes, I miss him. I've been with him for a month straight. I know he's gone away somewhere to work. He called me yesterday to tell me he was going to be gone for a few weeks. Wasn't that nice?"

"Yes, it was. You should come to my shop with me this morning. It smells so good in there."

"Do you make any strawberry cake at the bakery?"

"What kind of strawberry cake?"

"The kind with the creamy white frosting inside and on top with sliced strawberries on the top. It has to be refrigerated. I think the frosting is like Cool Whip, only thicker. It's my favorite and Luke's favorite also. We ate an entire cake in two days. I would love to order one of those cakes."

"We don't make those but I wonder if Austin knows how to make them," Julia said, writing down everything Missy told her about the cake. "I'll see if we can make this at the shop. Are you going to go with me?"

"I can't. I'm going to lunch with Riley. She found a new restaurant that opened and wanted us to go there today."

"I went with her last week. It is a great place. The décor is lovely. Kane and I went there last night. You'll enjoy it. Did Luke say where he was going?"

"No."

"Kane had to leave this morning, but he'll be back tonight. Does she stay in that same spot?" Julia asked, looking at Sheriff, lying on Missy's glass floor in her kitchen.

"Yes, she loves the glass floor. She jumps into the river. I have to towel her off all the time. She loves it here."

∼

Luke flipped through the file of papers in his hand, thinking about Missy. "Who is after this man? What's his name again?"

"His name is Greg Brown. He said his partner was going to have him murdered. He overheard him talking on the phone. He said he drove around and then decided to go home early and tell his wife. When he was heading to his house, he saw his wife get into his partner's car, and as he watched, they kissed each other."

"So, maybe it's both of them who want him dead. Damn, there are so many cheating bastards out there. Why get married if you are going to cheat? Tell your spouse, so they can at least get out of the marriage. Now this one wants to murder her husband. She probably also has an insurance policy on him. So how are we going to prove it."

Austin didn't say anything. He knew Luke's wife had cheated on him. She was with her lover when he stepped on a mine overseas and killed both of them. "The FBI will set them up. They'll put their feelers out there and see if they can find anything. We'll go to the safe house in Los Angeles. No one is there right now. So that will be good. I'm sure the guy must be depressed, knowing his wife and partner want him dead. His partner is his best friend, or should I say, he was his best friend."

"So he lives in Pittsburg. What excuse is he going to give them for not being around?"

"He said he always goes away for work, so it won't be anything new. If the FBI can get involved early on, then they'll say they killed him. They will have to show a photo of him dead. We'll take care of that. Then they'll arrest both the wife and the partner. Greg doesn't want them to know he's alive for a few weeks. He wants to see what they'll do first. I think he wants to make sure they are working together. A part of him can't believe his wife is in on this. That way, both of them will be charged for murder for hire."

"It's a shame you don't really know the person you marry until after you say the I do's."

"I didn't know Elie very long before we married. Sure, we had a fourteen-month-old baby girl. But it had been two years since we had seen each other. I knew I loved her the first time we were together."

"Yes, but Elie is Kane and Rory's sister, so you knew she came from honest people. When I married Susan, I was a fucking idiot. I had known her for three days and thought I knew her. I won't ever get caught up in that again."

"What about Missy?"

"She's my friend. We have never been together. I've never kissed her."

"That surprises me."

"Why?"

"Because you can feel the heat coming off the both of you when you are in the same room. I remember the first time the two of you met. I thought you were going to kiss Missy. Both of you took a step toward each other."

"Sometimes, you have to control your feelings and make better judgments. Missy is my friend. I don't want to mess that up. No matter how hard it is to keep from making love to her."

"Yeah, maybe she wouldn't want to make love to you either."

"Maybe," Luke said, looking out the window. His thoughts went to Missy. He wanted her more than he wanted any other woman, but he couldn't commit to marriage, and Missy only deserved someone who loved her and wanted to marry her. So that meant he needed to stay away from her.

∽

"Greg, it's time we take some photos." They had him lying on the ground on a country road. Ketchup was splattered all over the front of him. His eyes were open, and he looked like a dead man. "Perfect, I'll send these to the FBI, and they can share them with your partner. We don't know if your wife is involved or not. So we wait a few weeks and see what happens. How are you doing?"

"I feel like my world has blown up. I don't know what I'm supposed to do."

"When they show your partner your photo, they will have him on video. Your wife being told about your death will also be recorded. Because the FBI is involved, we do all of this their way."

"I understand. How could my wife do this to me? How can she just stop loving me? Why does she want me dead? Why not just divorce me. We've been married for ten years."

"Man, I don't know what to say. I'm sure if she is involved, she must have a large insurance policy on you. I'm most definitely the wrong person to ask that question to. Maybe she's not involved. We have to wait and see."

Two days later, they watched the look on Greg's partner's face when he was told about Greg's death. They watched as his wife put her hands over her face and grabbed the counter. Luke knew she was faking the minute he saw her. She planned her husband's murder right along with his partner. They would wait and see what happens. How long would it be before they started celebrating.

It only took one day for the partner to show up at her

house. The hidden camera showed them celebrating her husband's death. The FBI arrested both of them. Greg went home and sold their house and the business and moved as far from them as he could get.

The wife begged her husband to help her. He never even looked at her. Her parents and her sister never looked at her either. They were ashamed of her and washed their hands of her.

13

Luke wanted to see Missy. It'd been six weeks since he'd seen her. It felt like six years. He pulled his truck to a stop and sat there a minute. Luke watched the front door as Missy opened the door with a big grin on her face. He stepped out of the vehicle and walked up to where she was. He pulled her into his arms, and his lips locked onto hers.

Missy wrapped her arms around him. *Finally, he's going to make love to me.*

"This doesn't mean we are going to be together forever. If I want out, I'll tell you. If you think I'm going to fall in love with you, I'm not."

"Same here."

Luke nodded and picked her up, and carried her into the house. He went straight to her room and started taking her clothes off of her. Missy pulled his shirt off of him, and she was unbuttoning his jeans when his hand stopped her.

"What are you doing?" Missy whispered as he kissed her neck.

"I'll take them off." Luke picked her up, and they landed

on the bed together. Luke didn't want to do something wrong this first time, but he couldn't wait much longer. He took the rest of their clothes off and lay naked next to Missy. "Are you sure you want this?"

Missy didn't say anything. She pulled him down to her and kissed him as her shaking hands ran down his back. "This is all I want," she whispered in a feather-light breath that fanned across his ear. They made love for hours before both of them, exhausted, fell asleep.

WHEN MORNING CAME, Missy was happy to see Luke still in bed with her. She was ready for another round but she wasn't sure he was awake.

Missy gave him a poke and nothing. She was about to give him a harder poke when he grabbed her wrist. Before she could respond, he pulled her down on top of him. He wrapped his arms around her and rolled her onto her back. His knee nudged her legs apart, and he stretched out between her thighs, bracing himself on his elbows as he looked down at her flushed face.

Her heart raced. She went utterly still and waited to see what he would do. "*Don't let go*," she whispered to herself.

"I won't, Sugar."

She stopped thinking when she realized he heard her. Luke gently lowered himself onto her, his hard chest rubbed against her breast as he leaned over her to get a condom. They were stacked up next to his gun on the bedside table. When he began to nuzzle the side of her neck, shivers cascaded down her arms and legs. His breath was sweet and warm against her skin, and when he tugged on her earlobe, she felt a jolt of longing all the way down to her toes.

"This isn't a bad idea," she whispered as she tilted her

head to give him better access. She reached up, caressed his neck, and tugged on his hair. She wanted him to kiss her on her mouth.

He lifted up. "Want me to stop?"

"No," she reached up and kissed his chin. "No, I want you to kiss me."

She wished she would have kept quiet because now she was worried he'd stop touching her. She desperately wanted him to hold her and make love to her.

"Missy." His voice was a rough whisper against her skin.

Oh God, he was going to stop. She swallowed. "Yes."

"Open your mouth for me."

He didn't move. He waited for Missy to make up her mind. What he didn't know was she had made up her mind the moment she saw him.

Any worry about the consequences of their actions flew from her thoughts. There was only room for Luke. She stared into his beautiful eyes and pulled him to her.

It was all the encouragement he needed. His mouth settled on hers in a kiss that was warm and undemanding. And wonderful. But soon, it wasn't enough for him. One taste of her sweet mouth made him crave more. His tongue swept inside and rubbed against hers. He took his time leisurely exploring her mouth until that wasn't enough. He tightened his hold on her, and the kiss deepened.

With a groan, he lifted his head. "Tell me what you want."

"I want all of you."

The warm glint in his eyes made her shiver. His mouth swept across her lower lip. "You taste good, you know that?"

"Like sugar."

"Even better," he growled.

He was suddenly eager and hot, as though it was his first time. He knew how to please a woman—God knows he'd perfected his technique over the years—but this was different. This was Missy. The need to be with her made him ache. He'd never felt this way before.

Missy wasn't shy with him or hesitant. She stroked his back, his shoulders, his arms. He could feel her heart pounding, and when he touched her breast, she arched against him and moaned softly.

Her legs moved restlessly against his. He kissed the side of her neck and slowly moved lower, taking his time, teasing, tormenting her the entire time. His tongue gently tickled her collar bone, and at last, when he reached her breast, he felt her tighten around him.

He began to slowly drive her out of her mind. She had no idea her breast was so sensitive, but she lost a bit more control with each stroke of his tongue.

Luke was losing control as well. He took a deep, shuddering breath and passionately kissed her. His hands actually trembled. He kissed her again—hard, quick—then he pulled away.

"Be right back…." With a quick kiss, he rolled over. "I want to protect you."

Luke stood up to rip the condom out of the pack and put it on his hardened member.

One kiss, she thought, *and I melted.* She sighed. Luke certainly knew how to please a woman. No other man had ever made her feel the way he did. Not that she had many men. Two was how many she'd slept with.

She rolled onto her back, her gaze locked on his. His hands moved to her waist as he rolled her closer to him. He moved between her thighs and stretched. The view of him made her forget to breathe.

Her hands caressed his back, her touch feather-light until he kissed her again. Her touch quickly became more frantic. She clutched his shoulders, demanding he stop tormenting her.

"Luke." She didn't know if she shouted his name or sighed it. His hands had moved between her thighs, and he was driving her out of her mind. He knew just where to touch, exactly how much pressure to exert. She writhed in his arms, pleading with him to come to her.

She was desperate to feel every inch of him, to wrap herself in his warmth. His breathing became more labored, and that excited her even more. She would die if he continued to torment her.

Luke delayed as long as he could to give her as much pleasure as she was giving him. Her response made it impossible to wait any longer. He knew she was ready. His mouth covered hers, and he moved between her thighs and slowly sank into her liquid heat. She was so tight, so hot, he groaned from the sheer bliss. He stayed completely still inside her, panting as he whispered her name.

When he came to her, she cried out. The ecstasy was overwhelming.

"Ah, Missy," he breathed her name. "Damn."

She wasn't content to let him catch his breath. Every nerve in her body was clamoring for release. She lifted her knees to take him in deeper and began to move.

Oh, how she wanted to please him, to make him as crazed as she was. She bit his shoulder, kissed his mouth, and moved to his neck. She was panting now. He pulled back and thrust deep, and tears came to her eyes. She was staggered by the intensity of the feelings gathering inside her. His movements became more powerful, more all-consuming, more demanding. It was exquisite.

Even in the throes of raw passion, Luke had always been able to control his actions, to set his pace. But he couldn't control anything right now. He thrust into her again and again, powerless to slow down.

She was every bit as passionate as he. Tension built within her, ready to burst with the need for release.

Wave after wave of sensation poured over her. She let it sweep her away like a roller coaster plunging to the ground and jolting every nerve, the waves of pleasure coursing through her. She thought she might cry.

Luke kissed her, then buried his face in the crook of her neck, slow to recover, "Damn," he whispered.

A curse word…and yet, she felt as though she'd just been caressed.

He was panting against her ear. Or was that her panting? She was so shaken, she couldn't hold a thought. The man had turned her into a blithering idiot.

Missy didn't want to let go of him. Not ever. Crap, she knew she was screwed.

He rolled to his side and pulled her with him. Luke held her and stroked her, his touch tender now. Neither spoke, both content for the moment. The minutes ticked by, and she fell asleep in his arms. In the middle of the afternoon, she awoke. He was still there. Missy was surprised and content. She closed her eyes and went back to sleep.

When she woke up again, he was gone from her bed. Then she heard the shower. She threw her legs over the side of the bed and joined Luke. He smiled as he pulled her to him and made love in the shower; he kissed every scar on her back. He wanted to kiss away the pain she went through. They stayed in the shower until the water turned cold.

"Are you hungry?" Missy said, pulling her T-shirt down.

"Are you going to make breakfast?"

"Yes."

"Then I'm starving." Luke reached out and pulled her onto his lap. He kissed her until she was breathless. When their eyes locked onto each other, Luke bent and kissed her again. "Do I still get to eat?"

Missy smiled and stood up. She walked into the kitchen and wiped a tear from her cheek. *Damn, I love him so much. I can never love another man, not ever.* Sheriff was on the kitchen floor, staring at the river going by. When Missy bought the house, she loved the glass floor, but now it was hard to keep clean with Sheriff there. Between swimming in the river and running beside it, she continued to give him a bath every night.

14

"Hey, Luke, I have an assignment for you," Riley said, handing him a file.

"Thanks Riley. Where am I going?"

"New York. There is an ex-Army Ranger who needs you to be back up for him. He said he would talk to you when you get there."

"Hmm, I wonder why he didn't call on one of his buddies. I mean, the Rangers are all pretty crazy and mean. Why would he want us helping him?"

"Maybe he doesn't want his buddies to know he needs help."

"Maybe you're right. When do I go?"

"Ash is going to fly you there. You leave in thirty minutes. Sorry for the short notice, but I tried getting a hold of you. This was a last-minute assignment. Ash is your partner. I wouldn't send you in alone with a crazy, mean Army Ranger."

Luke laughed out loud. Then he stopped. He wouldn't have time to see Missy before he left. She was in Kalispell shopping with Julia. *Damn.* He'd call her.

"Are you ready?" Ash asked as he headed toward the garage.

"Let me grab my bag." He ran upstairs to get his bag and called Missy at the same time. It went to her voice mail. "Missy, I have to go out of town for a while. I'll see you when I get back."

~

Oh darn, I missed Luke's call. Don't call him back, Missy. He'll think you are clinging to him. He doesn't want me to become attached.

"So, what are you doing for Thanksgiving?" Julia asked as she settled the baby in the car. Then climbed behind the wheel.

"I'm going to the cabin. I'm going to Polly and Zane's for Christmas. I'm so used to just doing things on my own it's strange that Polly calls me all the time, wanting me to go and do things with them. It's not like we live in the same town. Now she wants me to move back to California."

"What do you want?"

"I'm staying here. I love my family, but we don't need to live in the same state."

"What about you. Do you miss living around Skye?"

"I do, but I'll never move back there. That was my past. Kane is my future. Plus, she's here all the time. I died in that car accident. The cartel would never leave me alone if I went back there. I don't want to ever go back to California."

Missy nodded. She knew how dangerous Julia's job as an FBI Secret Agent was. She almost died a few times. "That's true. Thanks for asking me to come along today. This was fun. Plus, I got to buy myself a couple of things."

"It was fun. Thanks for coming with me."

"Hey, we're besties. That's what we do. Bye, I'll see you later."

"See ya."

Missy walked inside, and the first thing she saw was Luke's T-shirt. She picked it up and hugged it to her and wondered if he knew how much she loved him. She hoped not. She tried not to show her feelings. She had to bite her tongue so many times before she told him she loved him. *I think I'll go to the cabin for a couple of weeks.* She packed some things and then made a reservation for the following day. *I believe I'll see if Sheriff can stay with Elie and Austin while I'm gone. She hates flying. Maybe I should drive. No, I don't want to drive that far away.*

"What do you think is up with this Army Ranger. I can't imagine his buddies not coming to his aid."

"I've been wondering the same thing. Why call a Navy Seal when you have the Army Rangers Special Forces?"

"We will find out soon. So what's up with you and Missy?"

"I'm not going to talk about Missy to you or anyone. My private life is my private life."

"Okay, I guess she knows what she's getting herself into."

"What would that be?"

"You don't have enough room in your heart for Missy. It's too full of Susan."

Luke shook his head. "You're wrong. Susan is no longer in my heart. I thought I loved someone who didn't really exist. Everything about Susan was fake. I've wasted five years mourning someone who only existed in my head."

"I'm sorry. I don't know what you are talking about, but I'm sorry."

"Yeah, me too."

They landed in New York. It was pouring rain. Their rental car was ready and waiting for them, so they headed out to see who their secret Army Ranger was. They drove for a while out of town before finding the Best Western motel.

Ash knocked on the door, and it was opened immediately. Both Ash and Luke grinned.

"Hello, Matthew Gray. Why are you in need of the Seal's?"

"Shhh, get in here. Hell, I don't want anyone knowing I called you. I need you because you can save people from the ocean, and we can't go by land."

"Go where?"

"To Iran, you can come in through the Gulf…"

Luke didn't let him finish. "Wait, why are we going to Iran?"

"We just got word that there is a Navy Seal held prisoner there."

"We haven't heard any of that."

"That's because we are there right now and have had contact. The problem is we can't get in through the Gulf. You Seals have the equipment. We don't."

"Who did they have contact with?"

"Alex Black."

"I heard he died two years ago," Luke said, looking at Ash.

"Same here. He must have survived. Has he been a prisoner this entire time?"

"Yes. So when do we go?"

Luke looked at Ash, "Day after tomorrow. We'll get everything ready. My God, can you imagine how happy his wife and children will be? Let me see the maps." Luke and Ash poured over the maps to see the best entrance getting in there and getting Alex out of there.

"I'm going to let Austin and Kane know and see if they want to join us," Ash said, taking out his phone.

"How is it no one knew about Alex being held prisoner? And why the hell did we have to come to New York to talk to you?"

Matthew laughed. "We had a bet whether or not you would come since it was an Army Ranger wanting help. Alex didn't tell the Iranians he was a Seal. He said they would have tortured him on video for his family to watch."

"How come you didn't get him out when you were there? And, of course, we would come. It's our job."

"That's what I asked. Why couldn't they bring Alex with them?"

"It would seem he's in a hot box that is sealed shut. So you'll have to take everything with you. I'm also going. Alex is my friend, and Kash will be going. He's the one who talked to Alex. We'll all have to go by water. They have more guards there now and have set up land mines all over the area. It's too dangerous to go by land. That's why I contacted you guys. If we could have done it without you, we would have. Nobody is to know about this until it's over. We don't want his family to get their hopes up."

"No one will hear about this from us," Luke said. He took out his computer and started configuring their route. "We'll have to be underwater for a long time. Then we'll have to go back the same way underwater. So we'll bring extra scuba gear with us. I hope he's not been hurt or beaten. How long has he been locked up in the hole?"

"He said he beat up the guard, and they threw him in there. I don't know how long he's been in the hole. The guard made a wise crack. I'm glad he's alive. His family will be thrilled. It almost killed his father when they told him Alex was dead."

"I remember that. Alex's brother kept saying he wasn't dead. He wanted to go find him that day. But the General told him to back off. He's on his way here. We haven't told him what's going on. He's still in the Army Rangers. If he wants to help, I say we let him. He can deal with his General when he gets back."

Luke pulled his hair back from his face. Then he tied it back with a piece of leather. "Yeah, I'm positive Jag will want to come along. I saw him about six months ago. He was fighting a guy outside of a club."

Someone knocked on the door, and Luke opened it.

"What the fuck are you doing here. I thought Matt called for this meeting?"

"Hello, to you too, Jag." Luke pulled the door open all the way. "Are you coming in?"

"What's going on here?"

"We're going on a mission. We thought you might like to come along."

Jag spotted Matt. "What's going on? Why would we go on a mission with the Seals?"

"We encountered someone when we were on a rescue mission. We need the Seals to help bring him home."

Jag sat down. "Is it Alex?"

"Yes."

"I knew he was alive. Damn. My father and Alex's family will be so happy. I'm going with you." Jag rubbed his hands over his face. "Thank God someone saw him. When do we go in?"

"We have to go by water. That's why we need the Seals. We can't tell anyone outside of this room about our mission."

"I won't say anything. Damn, my government could have had him out two years ago if they had listened to me. I just retired from the Rangers last week. So they can't lock me up for helping to rescue Alex. When do we go?"

Luke looked Matt in the eyes. "Day after tomorrow. You have to do as we say. We have to go by sea. There are too many land mines to go any other way. If I remember right, you have scuba diving knowledge. It'll be pitch black."

"Whatever you say. I have to cancel a few dates, and I'll be ready to go."

"Why, only a few dates. I would have thought you would have canceled at least ten."

"You are no one to talk about dates. If I remember right, you have left a ton of broken hearts in your wake."

"I'm not going to talk about the broken hearts I've left behind. But I never stayed around long enough for anyone to become attached." *Except with Missy.*

Matt shrugged his shoulders. "The same goes here with me. I never leave a broken heart behind." *There was only one woman, but she broke my heart.*

15

As soon as they were in the water, they knew this would be a dangerous trip. There were mines in the water for any boat that came through here. They could see them floating near the top. With their night headgear, they could see everything. It took them forty-five minutes to maneuver their way through the bombs and reach the shore, then they slipped out of their scuba gear and went the rest of the way on foot. Kash led the way. Two hours later, they were at the wall. Each one went up and over without making a sound.

They followed Kash to where Alex was held in the hole in the ground. That was precisely what it was, a hole in the ground. Luke put his fingers through the hole in the iron lid. They all worked together as fast as they could. They had the lid off and reached down to pull Alex out when a shadow walked past them. Luke turned and had the man by the throat. Luke never saw the knife that went into his side before he killed the guy. He didn't say a word to his buddies. They had to get the hell out of there before the other guards wondered where the guard was. Austin threw Alex over his shoulder, and they all left as one.

They were almost to the boat when the alarm went up. Luke could feel himself getting weak. He was losing a lot of blood. Hopefully, there were no sharks in the area. It took some doing for Luke to keep up with the others, but he managed until it was time to climb into the boat. He couldn't pull himself into the boat. Austin and Jag grabbed his arm and pulled. They were far out to sea, and still, no one talked. Voices carried on the water. Alex hit them a few times on the back to show how excited he was. He stared at his brother, who hugged him at least ten times.

Jag reached over and took his brother's hand. "Alex, I'm damn glad you're alive. Do you want to call your wife and children? We'll leave you alone."

"Thanks Jag, I would like that. Can you call Mom and Dad?"

"Yeah, I'll call them." Jag picked up his phone and made a call. "Hi, Dad."

"Jag, how are you, son?"

"I'm great. I have some news for you."

"Do you? I hope it's good news."

"It's the best news," he choked up, talking to his dad. So he cleared his throat. "Dad, we just rescued Alex. He was being held prisoner in Iran. He's on the phone with Tammy right now. We'll see you in a couple of days."

"What?" his dad was crying.

"I'll ask him to call you when he's finished talking to Tammy and the kids. I love you, Dad."

"I love you, son. I'm going to go tell your mother the wonderful news." His father was crying and could barely get the words out.

Jag saw Alex and Luke talking. He walked over to them. "What's going on?"

"Alex is getting cold feet about calling Tammy."

"I'm not getting cold feet. I just don't want to shock her. It's been two years. What if she's found someone else?"

"She hasn't found anyone, Alex. She's still morning you. Do you think one of us should call first and let her know in case she faints? Then I'll call her."

"Yeah, you dial the number and tell her I'm alive, and then I'll talk to her. I gotta tell you I'm really nervous about this. I feel like I'm going on my first date with her. Give me the phone, I'll do it."

Alex dialed her number. And when she answered, he held his heart.

"Hello, who is this?"

"Here," Alex tossed the phone to Luke.

"It's Luke Wilson."

"Luke, why are you calling me."

"You might want to sit down."

"Kids, quiet down. This is one of Dad's old friends. I'm sorry, what were you saying?"

"Why don't you put it on speaker, and the kids can hear also?"

She was puzzled but did it anyway. "Okay. Kids, come over here. We can all hear you."

"We rescued someone today. He would like to say something to you." They could hear her crying even before Alex said anything.

"Sweetheart, I'm coming home." The kids were screaming, and all of them were crying. No one could hear the other one talking. The guys got up, walked out of the boat's cabin, and let Alex spend time with his family.

Luke held his side and looked at the others. "Fuc..." Everything went black.

"What the hell happened to him?"

"Damn, he's got a hole in his side. The guard must have stuck him with his knife. We have to get him to the hospital."

"We are hours away from the nearest hospital. "Who has medic experience?"

"Alex does."

"Get him."

Alex shook his head as he looked at Luke's cut. "It's been a long time since I've done any medic work. Do you have a first aid kit?"

Ash got the kit, and they all watched as Alex cleaned out the cut. Then, he pinched the wound together and taped it closed. "We won't sew it up. It might get infected. I have no idea if anything major has been injured. Do we have any medication?"

"We have whiskey."

"Then whiskey will do. I wouldn't mind having a drink of whiskey myself right now."

Ash handed him the bottle, but he wouldn't take his eyes off of Luke.

Ash called Missy. "Hey, sweetie, I thought you might want to know. Luke was injured. I didn't know who else to call. I know how you feel about him."

Missy sat down on a stump. She had been running, but she stopped to answer her phone. She knew Luke and Ash were together. "How was he injured?"

"Do you remember Alex Black?"

"Yes, he died a couple of years back."

"He was alive. We rescued him. But Luke was stabbed when a guard walked upon us. None of us knew it until we got back on the boat. We're in Germany."

"Let me talk to him."

"Missy, he's still unconscious."

"Then put the phone next to his ear. I have something to tell him."

"He won't be able to hear you."

"I don't care if he can hear me. Put the phone next to his ear."

"Hang on. Okay, talk away."

"Luke, you listen to me. I want you to fight to stay alive. We have something good, and you know it. Don't you dare not wake up? Please try extra hard to live. Try for me, please."

"Missy…I…I'll be…fine," He murmured. Then he blacked out again.

"He heard you now he's out again."

"Call me, I'm at the cabin, but I'm leaving. What state will he be in?"

"He will probably be in Germany for a while."

"Then I'll see you in Germany."

"Missy, wait until we see how he is. We might be leaving before you get here."

"Did she listen to you?"

"She hung up on me."

Missy called Zane and Polly. She couldn't help it if her voice quivered while she was talking.

"Missy honey, I'll meet you at the Los Angeles airport," Zane said, trying to calm her.

"I'm sure Luke will be okay. Look how strong he is."

16

Missy ran into Zane's arms when she saw him. "Have you heard anything?"

"Yes, he has a fever, and he's still unconscious. They are moving him to a Belgium hospital. I've reserved tickets. We still have an hour before we leave. Let's go get something to eat. I'm starving."

"I'll take a glass of tea and a sandwich. I'm sorry I called you like a crazy person."

"Don't worry about it. We are going with Alex's wife, Diane, and their children."

"Oh my God, what a wonderful thing for this family. I'm so happy for them." The tears started, and they wouldn't stop. "I'm so happy for them." She couldn't stop crying.

Zane looked at her. He had never seen Missy cry. Even when the crazy killer was after her, she didn't cry. She didn't cry when she was beaten, that he knows of. She might have when she was alone. At least not in front of him. He took her hand, "Luke is strong. Once they get him some antibiotics, I'm sure he'll be fine."

"What if he wants to die. What if he wants to be with that cheating Susan."

"Missy, I have never seen you like this."

"I know. I can't help it. I love Luke so much. I'll stop crying. I'm sorry." Missy wiped her face off.

Zane stood up when he saw Diane and the kids walking and looking around. "Diane,"

"Zane, I can't believe Alex is alive. We are all so happy." She started crying. She looked over at Missy. They hugged each other.

"I'm so happy for your family, Diane. It's a miracle. Kids, I bet you can't wait to see your dad. He's going to be so happy to see all of you."

"Are you going with us?" Diane asked, looking at Missy. "What's going on? Why are you crying?"

"Luke has been injured. He's unconscious and has a fever. He'll be at the same hospital as Alex."

"Do you still love Luke?"

"Yes, more than ever. Don't say anything to him, though. I don't want to scare him off."

Diane smiled and took Missy's hand. "He would have to be crazy not to love you. You are as beautiful inside as you are out. I'm sure Luke already loves you."

"Thank you," Missy said, blowing her nose.

"Why hasn't he woken up yet?"

"Missy, the doctor said once his fever goes down, he should wake up. Why don't you go to the hotel room and get yourself some rest?"

She didn't want to hear that but she knew he was looking out for her. "I will. I need to shower and change my clothes. Call me if Luke wakes up."

"I will. Now go."

"How do you think he's doing?" Alex said, standing in the doorway with his arm around his wife.

Zane looked over at the door when he saw movement. "Aren't you supposed to be in bed? You need to eat a lot of food to get your strength back."

"They've allowed me to get up. I'm going home tomorrow. I first wanted to thank Luke, but I can see he's still unconscious."

"I'm glad you're getting to go home this soon. The doctor said as soon as Luke's fever starts going down, he'll probably wake up. Look, Alex, I'm sorry we didn't know you were held captive. If we had known, we would have gotten to you sooner."

"I know that. Hey, I'm thankful those Army Rangers found me when they did. I'm sure I'll be having nightmares for a long time. That's why I'll be talking to someone about it."

Missy tried sleeping. She thought for sure after her shower, she would fall asleep. She hasn't slept in four days except in that chair in Luke's room. *To hell with it.* She threw the covers off and got dressed. She put on her leggings and a cute top. She slipped her feet into her sandals. She grabbed her bag and walked to the hospital. It was only a few blocks from the hotel. She stopped and bought a couple of candy bars in case Luke woke up hungry.

She ran into Zane in the hallway. "Zane, go home. I will be fine here on my own."

Zane pulled her to him and hugged her. "Are you sure?"

"Yes, I'm sure. Go home."

He nodded once. "Okay, I'll go after Luke wakes up. The

others are in there visiting with him now. Why didn't you sleep?"

"I tried. But I couldn't."

"I'm going to get us all sandwiches and take them back to the room. I'll be back."

Missy walked into Luke's room and sat down in the only chair. She looked at Austin and Kane. "I hear Zane is taking food back to the hotel."

"Are you trying to get rid of us?" Austin asked.

"Yes."

"We'll see you later. We are only at the hotel. Call us if you need anything."

"I will. I'm sure I'll be fine."

Missy was almost asleep when she opened her eyes. Luke watched her. A tear slid down her cheek.

"Come over here, Sugar," he whispered as he raised the blanket, and Missy crawled in beside him. She couldn't stop the tears.

"I'm so happy you woke up," she whispered.

They fell asleep without a moment's notice. Neither could keep their eyes opened.

When Zane came to see how she was doing, Missy was sleeping, and Luke was awake, holding her in his arms.

"It's good to see you're awake. I'm going to head home. Tell Missy I'll call her."

"Where are we?"

"Belgium."

"Wow, I must have slept for days."

"You did. Missy hasn't slept anywhere except this chair. I'll tell the others you are awake. We were all waiting for you to wake up before going home."

"Thanks. I think I'll go back to sleep for a while."

After Zane left, Luke looked down at Missy. He was starting to get that trapped feeling. He didn't want to have that feeling. Luke knew Missy had strong feelings for him. He had strong feelings for her too, but he wouldn't ever get married again. He didn't want a relationship with someone who wanted them to be a forever couple. What if she wanted to go out with someone else, or he wanted to sleep with someone else. Luke decided he had to talk to Missy so she would understand why he won't ask her to marry him if that is what she wants. He closed his eyes and went to sleep.

When he woke up, Missy was gone. He almost panicked, but then he saw her standing by the window. "Hey." She turned and smiled.

"How do you feel?"

"Like I should get up and do something. Why are you still here? You don't have to stay with me."

"Hey, what are friends for? I don't mind staying until they release you. I'll fly home with you."

"Come and sit down."

Missy walked over and sat in the chair. "I know what you're going to say. You think I'm falling in love with you, and you want to warn me not to. Because I will only get hurt."

"I wouldn't put it that way. I just want you to understand I'm not going to get serious about anyone ever. I care for you, but I'll never get married again."

Missy smiled. "I know that. Why are you telling me this? We are fine, I promise. I heard you were here, so I came to be with you. It's no big deal. I didn't come here to get married. I came because you were injured. Stop worrying. I don't expect a marriage proposal because I'm here. I don't want to get married either. Not ever."

"Do you love me?"

Missy knew she looked sad as hell. She wanted to cry. "Since we are not going to be serious about each other. I don't think we can ask personal questions ever."

"That's fair. I'm starving."

"I'll go see what you can eat." She walked out of the room before he could say anything else.

Luke could see the sadness that came over her, and he hated that he did that. But it was better that she knew right now how it was going to be. He didn't want her to fall in love with him and become more hurt when he wanted out of the relationship. He didn't know if he would ever want out, but why wait for that time to come. If he could keep from hurting Missy, he would. She deserved someone who wanted a forever life with her, *Over my dead body. You can't have it both ways, Luke, and you know it.*

17

Missy and Kathy were having Thanksgiving dinner together. "This looks delicious. Thank you for having me for dinner."

"Are you kidding? I'm so happy not to be alone. Plus, I have all this food I ordered. When is the baby due?"

"In about three weeks."

"Kathy, you're staying here with me. I will not let you go into labor alone in your cabin. Have you talked to Marc about the baby?"

"Not yet. I don't know if I want to do that. Marc'll want to have my son in his life."

"You're having a boy. I'm so excited for you. Marc will make a great father. Kathy, please tell him."

"I will, but not today. I'll call him tomorrow. He probably doesn't even remember me."

"That doesn't matter. You have to think of your child."

"What are you going to do, Missy?"

"What do you mean?"

"What about your baby?"

"I don't have a baby."

"So, are you saying you're not pregnant?"

"Of course, I'm not pregnant. Why would you think I was?"

"Because you're tired, you eat those lemons like they are going to quit making them. But mostly because you get sick in the mornings."

"What? I can't be pregnant. Luke will think I got pregnant on purpose. What am I going to do?"

"Don't get upset, maybe I'm wrong. We'll go to town tomorrow and get a home test. I don't want you to worry. I took a home test when I thought I was pregnant, and they work great. I'm sure you aren't pregnant. I'm sure you have always loved lemons. And you probably just had a little bug. That's why you were sick."

Missy was shaking her head. She couldn't believe how blind she had been. Could she be pregnant? *It's been two months since that beautiful night with Luke. But he used protection every time... Except in the shower.*

"Here, I made you a plate of food. Eat this. Missy, you're starting to make me nervous."

"I'm sorry." Missy shook her head. "I almost had a heart attack there for a minute. I'm sure you are right. I had a bug. But I'm fine now. Let's enjoy our dinner."

They finished dinner, and Kathy headed home when the sun was going down. Missy cleaned the kitchen and went to bed early. She cried herself to sleep. *What am I going to do? Luke will never forgive me. He'll think this is a setup for him to marry me if I'm pregnant. He can't find out. I'll still go to Polly's for Christmas... I won't be showing. Then I'll come back here. If Kathy hasn't had the baby, then I'll stay here with her. Polly will understand.* Ten minutes later, Missy was sleeping. She didn't hear Luke drive up to her cabin. She didn't hear him enter her room. When he climbed into bed with her, she recognized him right away. Missy turned and cuddled close with him.

"Hey, Sugar, I wanted to be here for Thanksgiving with you. I'm sorry I'm late."

"You're not late," she whispered. "I'm glad you're here. Do you want me to heat some food up for you?"

"No, I stopped in town and got a hamburger." Luke pulled her into his arms and pulled her top off over her head. Then he took her bottoms off. When she was as naked as him, he started making love to her. Luke buried his face in her hair. He loved her feminine scent. Her skin felt so good rubbing against him. He wanted to touch her everywhere. Caressing her breast, he kissed a path down her neck, her whispered sighs urging him on.

Missy loved the way he stroked her, loved the feel of his hot mouth on her skin. When his hands made a path down her stomach and moved between her thighs, fire intensified before it became unbearable.

Their kisses became more ravenous, their caresses more demanding. Missy made him burn as no other woman had, and Luke could feel his control slipping. When he knew he could wait no longer before thrusting inside her, it was sheer bliss. Her hot heat surrounded him. The jolt of pleasure was so intense he thought her fire would consume him.

He stayed perfectly still inside her. Before he whispered, "You feel so good."

Her breathing was as ragged as his, her need as demanding. His lips kissed the base of her throat felt the frantic pulse of her heartbeat.

Missy wrapped her arms and legs around him to take him deeper inside.

Luke moved slowly at first, but then his control snapped. Their lovemaking was wild and passionate, and when they climaxed, she called out his name.

With a loud groan, he collapsed on top of her, pinning her to the mattress. He stayed there for long moments before rolling over and pulling her with him.

"Hey, Missy, I want to apologize for what I said in Belgium. I didn't mean for it to sound the way it did."

"Luke, please don't talk about it anymore. I want to lay in your arms tonight and not think of anything else."

Luke pulled her to him and snuggled up with her. He knew he screwed up when they were in his hospital room. He wanted to make it up to her. They both slept for a while before waking up and making love again and again. Missy was gone when he woke up. She left a note saying she was taking Kathy to her doctor's appointment. He walked outside and looked around. He started cleaning up around her cabin, where the storm from last week had blown in branches. An hour later, Missy pulled up. She looked different. He couldn't explain it even to himself. Luke just thought something was different. She walked to where he was and put her arms around him.

"I'm sorry I had to leave. I had already told Kathy I would be there. She had dinner with me last night. I'll heat us up some food. Are you ready to eat?"

"I'm starving. What have you been doing?"

"Nothing, I've been lazy for the last week. How long are you staying?"

"I was hoping you would go back with me."

"Kathy's baby is due in three weeks, and she has no one. I told her I would stay. Then I'm going to Polly's for Christmas."

"I have to escort a couple to Italy. They are scared that someone is trying to kill them. He won the Powerball and thinks a nephew is out to murder them."

"That wouldn't surprise me. People are crazy nowadays. So how long can you stay?"

"One more night."

"I'm glad you can stay another night. Luke, I don't want you to think you need to be with me. If you're going to be with other women, just tell me. We are still friends, and I hope we will always be friends even if we are no longer together."

"Are you not wanting us to be together?"

"No, I like us being together. I just don't want you to feel trapped with me. I'm a grown woman. I can handle almost anything."

Luke pulled her against him, "I want to be with you and no one else. Only you." He turned her around, "Okay?"

Missy nodded, "Okay, then let's finish off this food." They finished lunch, then walked out to the porch and sat on the swing.

"Do you feel safe here at night now?"

"Yes, I've actually met a lot of people, from what happened before. My neighbors bring me weapons."

"What kind of weapons?"

"One brought me a shotgun, one brought me a handgun and a large knife…You know, those kinds of things. They watch out for me."

"Do you know how to use them?"

"Yes, I have my own gun. I've carried a gun since I was kidnapped and beaten. I forgot to take it with me on my run the day that Shawn showed up. I wasn't thinking straight when I ran that day."

Luke frowned. He didn't like her being on her own. But he knew he didn't have a right to tell her what to do. "Be careful, whatever you do."

"I will. I'm trying to talk Kathy into staying here until after the baby is born. It worries me that she's by herself."

"Has she told Marc about the baby?"

"No, not yet."

"He has a right to know. Even if they aren't together, she should tell him."

"What if he wants to take his son from her claiming because she's gay, she has no rights."

"So she's having a boy. Marc would never take the baby from her, but it's his right to have a say in the child's life. You know how he is with family. I'm sure he would just have her move in with him."

"I'm pretty sure Kathy won't want to move in with him."

18

"Polly, I'm bringing my friend with me for Christmas. I hope that's okay."

"Of course, it is. Who is this friend?"

"Kathy had a baby two weeks ago, and I don't want to leave her alone. The baby was early, and Kathy hasn't been well since the birth."

"Bring them. I will have Zane put the crib up and in her room."

"Thank you. Will anyone else be there?"

"Marc and his sister, Mandy; Killian with Bird and the kids; plus Jonah and Rory with their child."

After Missy hung up the phone, she debated whether or not to tell Kathy that Marc would be there. She decided not to say anything. Marc had a right to know he had a child, just like if she had been pregnant, she would have told Luke. She felt like crying when she found out she wasn't pregnant. As crazy as that sounded, Missy couldn't help how she felt. She would be twenty-seven on her next birthday. Missy had feelings of becoming a mother. She thought maybe she should stop seeing Luke, or she would never meet a man she could love. But she also knew it wouldn't be fair to any man because she would never love anyone as much as she loved Luke. Maybe she could have a child from a sperm bank. She automatically shook her head. That didn't sound like something she would do. At least she now understood why Kathy got pregnant. She wanted a child before her youth was gone.

Missy picked Kathy up, and they drove to the airport. She looked over at Kathy because she was quieter than usual. She didn't look good at all. "What's on your mind?"

"I went yesterday to my doctor. He told me I have ovarian cancer."

"What, oh my God, what are you going to do?" Missy pulled over to the side of the road and hugged Kathy as she cried.

"I need to get a hold of Marc. Do you have his phone number?"

"Yes. Missy looked into Kathy's eyes. Marc is going to be at Polly's for Christmas. If you need to talk to him, he'll be there."

"I start my treatment in a week. I won't be able to take care of my baby while I have my treatment." She burst into tears and started weeping. Missy held her close unsure of the words to say to soothe her.

Finally she spoke, "Talk to Marc. He'll help you with everything. And I'm always here for you and the baby. Don't forget that."

"When are you going back to Montana?" Kathy sobbed.

"I haven't decided yet. I'm in no rush to get back home."

"What about Luke? He lives in Montana. I thought you loved him?"

"I do love him. I told you Luke doesn't want us to become a serious couple. He's worried I'll become attached."

"What an ass. I'm sorry. Maybe Luke will change his mind."

"It's not important. I'm more concerned about you."

"I'm going to take one day at a time. When I know my child will have a happy and safe life, then I can worry about what I need to do."

Missy pulled back out on the road with her thoughts on Kathy. *How can I feel sorry for myself when Kathy is going through what she's going through. I'm going to do whatever I can to help her.*

WHEN THEY GOT off the plane, they smiled as they took their coats off. It was seventy degrees in Las Angeles in December. "Wow, I do miss this beautiful weather. Oh, there's Zane."

"Hey sweetie, how are you?" Zane said, kissing her. "It looks like there is a glow about you."

"I'm good. I don't know about a glow," she laughed. "This is my friend, Kathy Reed, and her three-week-old son, Adam."

"Any friend of Missy's is a friend of ours."

"Thank you. I'm also a friend of Marc's. It's been a while since I've last seen him." She took a deep breath, "I'm going to introduce him to his son. He may have to raise him. I have stage four ovarian cancer, and I start my treatment in a few days. I've been wondering how to approach him about this. I was wondering if maybe you could talk to him. That way, when he sees his son with those beautiful green eyes of his. He won't be shocked."

Zane couldn't believe how blunt this Kathy person was being but he replied anyway, "I'm sorry you are going through all of this. Of course, I'll talk to Marc. I'm sure he'll want to do whatever he can for you. What about your family?"

"My family is crazy. They tried killing me because I'm gay and I was pregnant. They are locked up because of it, and my father was going to stab Missy. I would be dead if Missy didn't show up. When I met Marc, I knew right away it was him I wanted to have a baby with. I told him I was on the pill. Adam has Marc's last name. No one can take him from his father."

Missy patted Kathy's shoulder. "Kathy is a lawyer. She has taken care of everything. I told her she would be fine, and Marc would take care of everything."

"Yes, he will. Missy, you never told us someone tried to stab you."

"Luke was with us. He knocked Kathy's father out. So there wasn't anything to tell."

Polly was waiting at the door for Missy. She ran out and hugged her. "I missed you so much. Tell me what you've been doing?"

"I haven't been doing anything. Only a little stock exchange. This is my friend, Kathy Reed, and her son, Adam."

"I'm so happy to meet you, Kathy. Let me see this baby. Oh, he's so cute. Just watching him sleeping makes me want another baby." She heard Zane laugh and knew he would have something to say about that. "I have a room all ready for you and the baby. Let me show you where it is. Zane can bring up your luggage."

"Thank you." As they got upstairs, baby Adam opened his eyes.

"Oh my, he's beautiful." Polly picked the baby up and smiled down at him. "His eyes are the same color as Marc's eyes."

Missy changed the topic. "Your decorations are beautiful. I'm so happy to be here with my family. Where's Taylor?" Taylor was Zane's son, who he didn't know about until Taylor was thirteen. He had been in an abusive family.

"He has a girlfriend. I think he is serious about her. Don't say anything, but Zane checked her family out. They're good people."

"I'm happy about that. When will Zane stop investigating everyone we come into contact with?"

"Probably never. Polly tipped her head sideways. You look different. What have you done differently."

"I haven't cut my hair. While I'm here, I'll get it cut. In fact, I'm going to make an appointment right now."

"It's not your hair. I guess it's that the older you get, the more beautiful you become."

"Thank you, I look just like you."

Polly laughed and put her arm around Missy. "I've missed you. You have to visit us more. It's easier for you because it's only one person. If we visit you, we have to pack up everyone and all of their things. It's a lot of work. I talked to Julia, she said she hasn't seen you much lately."

"No, I haven't been home. I wanted to stay at the cabin with Kathy so she wouldn't be alone when she had the baby."

Someone knocked at the door. Before Polly could answer, Zane and Marc walked in. "Hello Missy, how are you doing?"

"I'm good. Kathy and the baby are upstairs."

"Marc, Kathy's son, has eyes that look just like yours," Polly said. Then she looked at her husband, and he shook his head. "Wait, are you telling me Adam is Marc's son?"

Marc took the stairs two at a time.

"Yes, he's Marc's son. I'll explain everything to you later. Kathy isn't well, so Marc is going to try and talk her into staying with him. She has to start chemo soon."

"Oh, the poor thing. Marc will take care of everything. No wonder he looked so much like Marc."

19

"So, Marc has a baby, and he moved Kathy and the baby into his house?"

"Yes, the baby is Marc's. He looks just like his daddy. One look, and you know he belongs to Marc. He's so precious. Poor Kathy is starting chemo treatments tomorrow. She is really sick. The doctor in L.A. didn't hold out much hope for her. He said women with ovarian cancer don't have a long life span. Marc is taking care of everything for her. I'm so happy she met me, and I knew Marc."

"Oh, that is so sad. I hope Kathy makes it."

"Me too."

"Are you here to stay now."

"Yes, for a while anyway. I have a lot of work to do. I'm building another computer site for a company. I've already sold it. Now I have to build it."

"I could never do that. It would give me a headache looking up all those little numbers."

"Julia, I can remember you looking for hours on the internet for underground cartel work. You would do just fine." Missy smiled at her friend. "I'll see you later. I'm so tired I'm about to drop."

"Are you coming down with something?"

"I don't know. I made an appointment with a doctor in Kalispell. I think I just need some vitamins."

"Well, you take care of yourself. Oh, here, I have some chicken noodle soup you can take home."

"No, no. I bought myself a bunch of that stuff. But thank you, anyway. Bye Julia."

"Bye."

"Well, you don't have a bug." Doctor Maria Lopez said, smiling at Missy. "But you do have something. You have a baby in there. I'll start you on prenatal vitamins. That will pick your energy up." The doctor looked at Missy, "Are you okay?"

"What? Did you just say I am pregnant?"

"Yes, does that surprise you?"

"I took a pregnancy test two months ago. It said I wasn't pregnant."

"Well, it was wrong. I believe you are around five months pregnant."

"Five months! I only have four more months until my baby is here? How could I not know?"

"Have you had a menstrual period?"

"I'm never on time, but I have had a few light periods."

"Sometimes that happens. Are you not happy about the baby? It's too late to abort it."

"What, no, I would never abort my baby. I love my baby," Missy started crying. She couldn't help it. She needed to talk to someone. She didn't know what she was supposed to do. Her baby was inside her.

"Do you want to know what you are having?"

"Yes, yes, I need to see my baby."

"Wait right here. I'll be right back."

Missy sat up on the table. She had to talk to Luke. She would call him tonight. *What's he going to say? Will he think I got pregnant on purpose? Who can I talk to about this?*

A nurse came in pushing a machine, "If you lay back, I will get this all hooked up. This is going to be cold," the nurse said, squirting some gel on missy's tummy. Missy didn't care how cold it was. She watched the screen as the nurse rolled the camera around on her stomach.

"There you go. See, that's your baby's face. I'll print all these pictures out for you. Do you see what I see?"

Missy knew the tears were running down the side of her face out of both eyes. She couldn't help it. She saw her baby moving, and she could feel it. "No, what do you see?"

"I believe I see a baby boy."

Missy saw him when he turned. Then as she watched him stretch, she felt his foot push her stomach. Missy laughed. She could feel every movement now. She was so happy she couldn't stop the tears that fell down her face.

"Oh, brother, I'm like a faucet I can't shut off. Can you please print two of those out for me? I have to give his daddy one of them. I'm so happy. I don't think I've ever felt this much love before. Well, I have a ton of things to do. I live on the river. I'll have to sell my home and buy a safer one. Thank you for showing me my baby." Everything came out all at once almost in a rumble. Missy walked out of the office in a daze.

"I'll have these printed out, and you can go up front and get your next appointment set up."

"Okay, thank you."

Missy stopped at the safe house. She had to talk to Luke. She didn't even know where he was. When she pulled into their driveway, she noticed there were a lot of cars there. Maybe she didn't want to talk to Luke yet. She would go and see who was there. She opened her door when she saw Austin walk outside, followed by Kane.

"Hey, long time no see," Austin said, hugging Missy.

"Yeah, I've been pretty busy."

"Hey, Missy. How are you doing?"

"I'm doing fantastic. Is Riley here?"

"Yes, she's inside."

"It looks like there are a lot of people here. Maybe I'll come back later."

"A few of the Army Ranger Special Forces are here. They are leaving. We helped them with another rescue. Go inside."

"Is Luke around?"

"No, I don't know where he is. He took some time off."

"Oh, I'll say hi to Riley. Then I'll get going. I have a ton of stuff to do."

"We'll see you around."

"Missy walked inside, looking for Riley. She went straight to Riley's office."

"Hi Missy, it's so good to see you."

"Hi Riley, how are you doing?"

"I'm doing good, keeping busy. I've been thinking about joining the service."

"What, why would you do that?"

"Well, I'm working with all these men who are making a difference."

"Wait, how do you think they make this difference? It is because you are their General, you tell them where to go and what to do. That's you. If you only knew how many times I've wanted to be you. You do something meaningful. I don't."

"Thank you. You are always doing something meaningful."

"Thank you..." Missy blushed but was very distracted now. "Do you know where Luke is?"

"He's taken some time off. Ryes told me he met some woman he knew in the service, and they went away together. He didn't know where. I called Luke, but I couldn't get a hold of him. Ryes said he was going to an island somewhere and would be back in a week."

"Hmm, I wonder what is going on. I hope everything is okay."

"I'm sure it is. Now, tell me why you look like you are about to burst."

"It's nothing; I'm just glad to be home. I have a lot to do, so I better get going." Missy worried about Luke. She wondered why he would have to go to an island with a woman. It never dawned on her that Luke found someone else. She knew he would tell her if that happened. Oh well, I'll let him know when he gets home. She called Harold to see what he was doing.

"Hi Missy, I'm glad you're back. I have something to tell you."

"What is it?"

"I got a scholarship to go to the University of Montana."

"That is wonderful. I'm so proud of you. Congratulations. What are you doing tonight?"

"I have a date."

"What? Congratulations again."

Harold laughed. "Thank you. I'll come by tomorrow."

"Sure, whenever you want, I'll see you around."

Missy drove home with a smile on her face. She would have dinner with her son. She has never needed people around her. She wouldn't start needing that right now. Sure she wished someone was here to share her wonderful news with, but she'd tell them when she saw them. This baby was no secret. She planned to tell all of her friends her wonderful news.

20

Luke was angry. No, angry wasn't the word he would use. He was so fucking angry he felt like he could murder someone. If Elizabeth was lying, she would get an ear full from him. When he saw her overseas, and she told him what she did, you could have hit him with a feather and knocked him over. How could Susan have had a baby without him knowing about it? Sure they were apart a lot, but a baby took nine months. He knew she could have done it. Some women don't show for a long time. She did visit her mother for a long time. She said she had to take care of her mother, that the doctor said she was dying. He now knew that was most likely another one of her lies, since his daughter was supposedly living with her grandmother.

"Why would no one try and get a hold of me?"

"I don't know. All I know is when I was here, I saw Susan's mother and a little girl who the mom said was Susan's child."

"Why the hell didn't you call me?"

"Nobody knew where you were."

"Yeah, that was my crazy time when I thought I had lost

the love of my life. I found out that she was cheating on me the entire time we were married. How am I supposed to know if this is my baby?"

"Because she did a DNA when the baby was born and found out she wasn't her boyfriend's child. So Susan left her with her mom."

She was a worse bitch than I thought she was. Damn, I hope the grandma doesn't try to fight me over this. My child is coming home with me. I should have called Missy. I'll call her when we get there. I wonder how she is. I never thought I could miss someone as much as I miss her. I hope my daughter likes me. I can't believe Susan didn't tell me I had a child.

When the plane landed, Luke walked down the aisle behind Elizabeth. The heat hit him in the face. He looked around at the place where his daughter lived. It was hot. Puerto Rico. Hell, he didn't even know Susan came from Puerto Rico. She told him she grew up in Miami, Florida. Another lie. They rented a car, and Elizabeth told him the way. He drove out of town until they came to a neighborhood that was run down. Skinny dogs ran everywhere.

"This place has really gone downhill. It doesn't even look the same. Turn up here." Luke had barely turned into the street when Elizabeth blurted out, "There it is. See that little girl, that's her."

Luke stopped and watched the little girl playing in the dirt. She had on a dirty dress. Her hair wasn't combed. It hung down her back in tangles. She was barefoot and looked to be having the time of her life. She bossed the other kids, and they did whatever she said. "She's beautiful even with all that dirt on. Her hair is the same color as mine. Well, I guess it's time I said something to her." Luke was nervous. He wanted his daughter to like him, because he already loved her.

"Hello."

The little girl looked up at him and ran inside the house. "Grandma, my Dad's here."

"It's about damn time." She opened the screen door and looked at Luke. "Yep, you're her Dad, alright. Her hair and eyes look just like yours. So what took you so long?"

"Elizabeth told me about her yesterday."

"Why didn't Susan tell you about your daughter? Never mind, Susan only cared about one person, and that was herself. Well, come in and meet your daughter."

Luke stepped inside. Elizabeth walked in behind him. He could actually feel himself shaking. He was so nervous for his daughter to like him. He looked around at the rundown shack and was furious that Susan would leave her daughter to be brought up in this place. He watched as the little girl walked out of a back room. She tried to clean herself up. She washed her face, but that only made the dirt smear more on her. She changed her dress. Now she wore a pink frilly dress that dragged on the ground. It was way too big for her. He thought she was beautiful.

"Hello, can you tell me your name?"

"You don't know my name. I'm your daughter. You're supposed to know my name."

"I just found out I had a daughter yesterday."

"Oh. My name is Addison, but everyone calls me Addy. My grandma named me. My no-good mother didn't care if I had a name or not. Isn't that right, Grandma?"

"That's a beautiful name," Luke choked out.

"Thank you. Am I going home with you?"

"I'm hoping you'll want to go with me."

"Yes, because grandma is going to live with my uncle, but he didn't want any kids living there. He's not very nice, but my aunt is nice to me. Grandma is getting old. She can't keep taking care of me. I think I'm going to miss my grandma."

"You can always visit your grandma."

"See, Grandma, I told you he would let us visit. My Uncle lives in Oregon."

"I live in Montana. You can visit your grandma whenever you want."

Luke looked around the place and wondered what his daughter wanted to take with her.

"We'll leave tomorrow. You can pack your things and tell Grandma goodbye. I have a room at the hotel. We'll go shopping for clothes after you say your goodbyes."

"Thank you for coming to get Addy. I was so worried that you wouldn't come for her. She'll be seven on her birthday."

"I would have been here on the day she was born had I known about her. I love my daughter. I will do anything for her."

"You love me."

"Of course, I do. You're my daughter. I've loved you since I found out about you."

"No one ever told me they love me."

Luke could feel himself getting angry again. Why had no one told Addy they loved her? "Well, you better get used to hearing it because I'll be telling you all the time how much I love you."

"I have to pack all my things."

"Would you like me to help you?"

"Yes, thank you."

Luke followed her to the back room, where a tiny bed was set up along the wall, and a little dresser pushed up against the other wall. His daughter slept in the hallway. The only other room was a tiny bedroom big enough for a twin bed, and a small bathroom. The place looked like it would blow away with just a little wind, not to mention the hurricanes that came through here.

"When is your birthday?"

"In two weeks."

LUKE

Luke was shocked. How could Susan have done this to her own blood, her own child? He kept his anger at bay. "We'll have a party for you. Would you like that?"

"Are there any kids where you live?"

"Sure there is. You can meet lots of kids when you start school."

"I don't go to school. It's too much trouble for grandma to try to find me a ride, so I stay home. Grandma has been homeschooling me, and she doesn't like it one bit. She said she would be glad when she's rid of me. She said my mother was selfish. Was my mother selfish?"

"One day, I'll tell you about your mother. Even though we were married, I didn't really know a lot about her. We weren't around each other that often. Do you have a suitcase?"

"No, I'll get a bag for us." Addy came back with a small cloth bag that had holes in it. "These are small on me, but I'll take them anyway. Grandma said she could make me some other clothes with them."

"Why don't we go shopping and buy you more clothes when we get home?"

"You don't think that would be wasteful?"

"No, I don't think that at all. Is there anything special you want to take with you?"

"Only my picture of you." She raised up her little mattress and pulled out a crumpled photo of him.

"Let's tell your grandma goodbye and go to the hotel." Luke walked back into the room where the grandma sat with Elizabeth. "Thank you for taking care of Addy. Here you go." He handed her an envelope with money in it. She looked in the envelope and swayed.

"Thank you. Goodbye, Addy, you be a good girl for your daddy."

"Bye, Grandma." There were no hugs or tears. Just goodbye.

Luke knew right away his daughter never got any hugs or kisses. No one ever told her they loved her. He would make sure that all changed when she was with him. He wished his mom would have known his daughter. "Have you had lunch yet?"

"No, I don't usually have lunch."

"Why don't we order something when we get to the hotel. Are you hungry?"

21

Missy looked around at the baby's room. She had Theodore paint it sky blue. Today Harold helped her put up the furniture. She was delighted with the outcome. Julia wanted to help her, as did Elie. But she had already finished. She went shopping for baby clothes and called Kathy to fill her in on what was happening. She got ahold of Marc.

"Kathy is in the hospital. The doctor said she only had a couple of days left. She is in a coma because of the pain medicine they are giving her."

"Oh no, poor Kathy. I wish I had been there with her. She doesn't have anyone."

"She has me. I am here with her. I have the baby with me. We will be here until the end. There is nothing anyone can do."

"I know, it's so sad. Thank goodness I knew you, and Adam has his daddy."

"Yes, it is sad. I thank God every time I look at my son that you knew Kathy."

After the call, Missy was again left alone with nothing but

her thoughts. She wished Luke was with her, that he knew she was pregnant, that he would be feeling their baby kick inside her. Missy went out and sat on the deck looking over the river. She would have to find another house. This one is not safe for kids. When her phone rang, she looked at the caller I.D. "Luke, how are you?"

"I have so much going on right now. I'm in Puerto Rico. I found out I have a daughter. She has been living with her grandma in a two-room shack. Susan didn't even tell me I had a child. She lived in a run-down part of town. The poor thing didn't even have clothes to wear that fit her. Her name is Addison, but she likes to be called Addy. She'll be seven in two weeks. I'm still in shock over finding out I have a child. I'm going to make sure Addy knows I want her, so I might not be around much. I'm going to focus all my extra time on my daughter. As soon as I have a chance, I'll visit you. I miss you." He didn't allow her to get a word in. He finally finished.

"That's wonderful that you have a daughter. I understand why you would want to focus all your time on Addy. Don't worry. We aren't in a must-see relationship. I mean, it's been a few months since I have last seen you. I don't understand why you're calling to tell me why you can't be with me? You don't owe me any explanations. We are both free to go our own way. Please don't feel you have to call me and explain anything to me."

"Missy, the reason I'm calling is that I won't be able to go to you. I'll have my daughter with me, and I'll have to stay with her at night. I want you to understand I want to be with you, but I won't be able to stay overnight because I have Addy. Yes, I do have to explain to you what's going on. I care about you."

"You don't have to explain anything to me. We don't have a relationship that says we need to explain to each other why we aren't able to see each other. But I'm glad you called me."

"The hell we don't. I want you to know why I can't be with you. I want to be with you, but I have to be with my daughter. She has never had anyone tell her they love her. She has never had anyone hug her. When I offered to buy her clothes, she said, 'Isn't that wasteful?' Can you imagine that? Those were her exact words. She has never had clothes of her own. The neighbors are the ones who gave her used clothes.

"Missy, you mean something to me, and I want you to know why I can't see you like before I left. I can't stay all night with you because my daughter needs me to show her how much I love her."

"Luke, it's okay. I understand. Don't worry about it."

"Wait. I might have worded that wrong. I still want you in my life. I'll still see you, I promise. Please don't ever think I don't want to be with you."

"I have to go. I have a cake in the oven."

"Missy, don't hang up yet."

"My cake will burn. Goodbye, Luke."

LUKE KNEW he messed that conversation up. He would go see her when he got home and explain things better. He looked in on Addy sleeping. She was so surprised when they went into the clothing store. She picked out pink and green and purple and every other color of dresses. She didn't buy any jeans, only dresses. She bought three pairs of shoes. She wanted to purchase a pair of women's red high heels, but the woman who helped her talked her out of it.

When they got to the hotel, she took a bath for the first time in her life. Luke insisted she shampoo her hair. It took a lot of hair conditioner to get the tangles out but he combed them out himself to make sure they were all gone. She also watched the TV for the first time. He went to bed and fell asleep with Missy on his mind. He loved Missy, but that was something he would never admit to her or anyone. Luke would never marry. He couldn't live through something happening to Missy. He knew that didn't make a lot of sense.

THEY LANDED in Montana and Luke hired a taxi to drive them home. He needed to rent an apartment soon. He would start looking around tomorrow. He was going to see Missy before he did anything. He would introduce her to Addy. Luke hoped they liked each other because they would be seeing a lot of each other.

"Hello, Riley. Are you here?"

"I'm in the kitchen."

Luke walked into the kitchen where Riley was cooking dinner. "That smells delicious."

"Who do we have here?" Riley said, looking at Addy.

"Riley, this is Addy. She is my daughter."

"Wow, you have a daughter?" Riley said looking puzzled. "She's beautiful. Have you talked to Missy?"

"I'm going to go see her."

"Oh, she's not at home. Her friend Kathy died."

"That's horrible. How did she die?"

"She had cancer. Marc has his son. He's going to raise him alone. I mean, he might meet someone. But for now, he will raise him alone."

"I'll call her later. I'm going to give Addy a spare room until I can rent a place."

"Of course, why don't you put her in the room next to yours? It also has its own bathroom. It's so nice to meet you, Addy. You're going to like living in this town. Everyone is so friendly."

Addy nodded, but her eyes were on the pool outside. "Can I go swimming?" she asked Luke.

"Do you know how to swim?"

"Yes, I swam in the ocean all the time."

"Sure, you can swim whenever you want," Luke said, smiling at her.

"Thank you," she walked out back and pulled her dress off over her head, and jumped in.

"You might want to buy her a swimsuit," Riley said, watching the little girl swim. She stayed underwater for the longest time. "She can stay under longer than the Seals."

"She sure can," Luke said, smiling. "I didn't even know she can swim. She had a very lonely upbringing. I'm going to change all of that. But first I'll take her shopping tomorrow. She didn't have any clothes, I bought her some in Puerto Rico, but I forgot the swimsuit. I had no idea she would take her dress off. I don't know anything about little girls. I guess she will also need under ware and things."

"It's my day off tomorrow. I can go with you if you want, that way you'll know what to buy. That dress is way too big for her."

"She had that already. She loves it. She wouldn't let me get rid of it. She likes the frills on it. We would like it very much if you came with us. I'm going to get Addy a towel and call Missy. Dinner smells delicious. Are we the only ones here?"

"Ryes is here. I swear that man is crazy. He went grocery shopping with me, and the butcher asked me out. Before I could answer him, Ryes told him I couldn't go out with him. Can you believe that?"

"Did you want to go out with him?"

"No, but I wanted to tell him myself. Ryes didn't know if I wanted to go out with the man or not."

"Riley, the guy was old enough to be your father. There was no way in hell I was letting you go out with the guy… Is there a little mermaid in the pool?" Rye said then he ran outside and jumped in as Riley and Luke watched. He pulled Addy out of the water.

"Ryes, what are you doing with my daughter?" Luke demanded.

"Hell, she wasn't coming up for air. Your daughter? Since when have you had a daughter?"

"Since I found out about her two days ago."

"She can stay under longer than the Seals," Riley said, smiling.

"Really," Ryes looked at Addy. "So, you're Luke's daughter."

"Yep."

"Did you know Luke was your dad?"

"Yep."

Ryes looked at Luke. "Did you know you had a daughter?"

"No, I did not. But when I found out, I went and got her. She will live with me from now on."

Ryes looked at Addy, who jumped back in the water. She was like a fish. "Where did you learn to swim?"

"In the ocean."

"Who taught you."

"I taught myself. When I was little, I went to the ocean and I walked into the water. I kept walking when a wave came up and caught me. It took me out to sea. I was scared, but I knew I had no one to help me, so I started swimming. I stayed under for a long time. I knew if I swallowed the water, I would die. I floated on my back for a long time. I was way out when someone pulled me out of the water. It was a fisherman. He took me to my grandma and told her she needed to watch me better. She called him a stupid ass and kicked him out of our yard. After that, I went to the ocean all the time."

Luke shook his head. "Don't say bad words."

LUKE

"What are bad words?"

"Stupid ass is a bad word. You lived too far from the ocean to walk there every day."

"We used to live near the water, but the hurricane tore our house down. So we had to move. Sometimes I would jump on the back of a truck, so I could go to the ocean and swim in the water."

"God, she's worse than Austin about the ocean. I wish Killian was here to see her swim. He would be stunned. I mean, no one can stay under longer than Killian until now. Your daughter can stay under longer than him. Did your grandma let you go alone? Who watched you?"

"Yes, I was a nuisance to grandma. She got stuck with me when I was left at her house by my selfish mother. Who only loved herself."

"I'm going to have to talk to her about not repeating everything her grandmother said."

Ryes shook his head. "I can't get over a child going to the ocean alone."

"My grandma said she wished I would drown, but I came home every night. She would be so angry she would lock me outside all night. I would sleep on the porch with the neighbor's dog."

Luke looked at her, petrified at what he'd just heard but didn't want to frighten her. "I have a dog. He's in the kennel right now. We'll get him out tomorrow. He sleeps inside the house. And that's where you will sleep, inside the house." He looked at his friends, "Addy didn't have a good life. But now she will have one," Luke said, he was so angry he wanted to put his hands around the grandma's throat and squeeze.

Ryes wanted to know more about Addy and the ocean. "Have you ever surfed?"

"Yes, I had my own surfboard. I found one thrown away.

When Jorge saw me dragging it, he gave me my own board. I kept it at the hut. I didn't want my grandma to see it."

Riley looked at the little girl like she just met a superstar. "Would she be worried you would hurt yourself?"

"No, she would sell it. That's what she did. Someone told her about me surfing in the ocean, and she took it away from me and sold it."

"I'll buy you a new one," Ryes said. "We love surfing."

"Do you love surfing?" Addy said, looking at her dad.

"Not as much as Ryes and Austin, but yeah, I enjoy surfing. When we go to California, we'll go surfing together."

"Now it's time to get out of the water and wrap up in this towel. We'll have a talk about swimsuits as well. Young ladies don't take their clothes off to swim."

"Why not. If I don't take my clothes off, then I'll get my dress all wet."

"We're going to get you a swimsuit. We'll get you three swimsuits. That's what you will wear from now on when you go swimming. How old were you the first time you went to the ocean by yourself?"

"I was three. That was a long time ago."

"Yes, it was. Follow me. I'm going to get you some bath water started."

"You mean I get to take another bath?"

"You can have a bath every night."

"Every night."

"Yes, every night."

Riley and Ryes stood there watching them walk away. "I wonder what he will say when he sees Missy," Ryes asked.

"I don't know," Riley said, "but if I know Missy, she will want to take care of this little girl. I hope Luke doesn't shut her out. We can't tell him anything about the baby. Missy made all of us promise."

"Yes, she did."

LUKE

"I don't know why."

"Dinner smells great. What are we having?"

"It's something my mom taught me to cook. Lasagna, with garlic bread and salad."

"I love lasagna."

"You love everything."

"Yes, I do," he said, looking at her.

Riley could feel her face turning red. She has always had a crush on Ryes. He was so handsome she knew she would never have a chance with him. He had so many women friends. And none of them looked like her. They were all beautiful with long legs and sleek, beautiful hair. Riley kept hers in a ponytail, and it was two different colors right now.

22

Missy had just gotten home when she heard a vehicle and turned around. Luke and his daughter pulled to a stop. Missy smiled and met Luke at his truck door. As soon as he opened the door, he pulled her into his arms and kissed her. "I missed you, Sugar."

"I missed you too. Are you going to introduce me to this beautiful young lady?"

He opened the back door and helped Addy out. "Addy, this is Missy. Missy, this is Addy."

"Hello, Addy. I'm so happy to meet you. My goodness, your eyes are just like your daddy's. Why don't you come inside? I have just gotten home, so I need to get my bag out of my car."

"I'm sorry about Kathy. I had no idea she was sick. I feel so bad about her death, just having the baby and all. Luke said taking out Missy's bag for her."

"Yes, it was so sad. When she had her baby was when they found out she had cancer. She went faster than I thought she would. Marc took care of her and his son."

Luke took her bag and carried it inside for her. His other

arm he put around her and pulled her into his side. "Riley said you were helping Julia with the bakery."

"Only for three days, she has a teenager coming in after school helping her now. Would you two like something to drink? Why don't we order Pizza? Have you guys eaten yet?"

"No. What do you say, Addy, do you like pizza?"

"I've never had pizza. It sounds good."

"You'll love it," Missy said, watching the little girl. "I'll be right back." She looked around for her bag, then she realized Luke must have taken it to her room. She took her phone out of the bag and called a pizza in.

"Do you swim in the river?" Addy asked, staring at this beautiful woman who her dad liked.

"Not in this area. It's way too swift. But there is a place to swim further down the river. Do you like to swim?"

"She is a fish in water. Addy loves swimming," Luke said, walking into the kitchen. "But you can't swim here. If you want to swim, you can swim in the pool." Luke wanted Missy and Addy to like each other. But it seemed like they were both uncomfortable. "Missy just got back from California."

"You did. Do you know how to surf?"

"Yes, I do. Not as good as some of my friends, but I love surfing."

"Do you have a surfboard?"

"Yes, I have two, a short one and a long one. Do you like to surf?"

"Yes, I love surfing. But my grandma sold my surfboard."

"Was she worried you would drown or something?"

"No, she wanted me to drown. She sold it because she wanted the money."

Missy couldn't believe what Addy said. "What do you mean she wanted you to drown?"

"Grandma said I was a lot of work for her, and I should be

lucky she took care of my ass. She told me she wished I would drown, so she didn't have to take care of me."

"What other mean things did she say or do? I'll get you some cookies and milk while you tell me everything."

"Okay. My grandma got stuck with me because I had her blood in me. My no-good mother dropped me off with her when I was born."

"Wait, I thought Susan was a nurse?"

"I thought so too. Susan lied. She worked at a nursing home before she joined the Navy. I understand she was supposed to go up for fraud when she died."

"I'm so sorry. Are you okay?"

"I'm fine. Now that I know how she was. I wish she would have been a good mother for Addy, but I realized I didn't know anything about Susan. She was fake, all of her."

Missy looked at Addy. "Whatever your grandma told you, I want you to forget everything she said to you. You are so very special. One thing your grandma did right was to keep you until your daddy found you. You are a sweet, beautiful little girl. Your daddy is so proud of you. You have brought him so much happiness."

Addy looked at Luke. "Did I bring you happiness?"

"Yes, sweetheart, you do bring me happiness." He looked at Missy, and she wiped tears from her eyes.

Addy looked at Missy. "Are you crying?"

Missy laughed. "Yes, I'm sorry, I'm just so happy Luke found you."

"I never cry. Grandma would give me something to cry about. Once I almost cried and she knocked me off my feet."

Missy reached over and hugged her. Then she took her hand and kissed it. She kissed her cheek. "I'm glad we are friends."

"You are?"

"Yes, I am. The pizza is here. Wait until you taste it."

They were all eating. Missy and Luke watched as she took her first bite. She was chewing and talking at the same time. "I love this… I want to have it every night."

"We aren't going to have it every night. But we can have it once a week."

"Okay. Do we live with Riley and Ryes?"

"That's where we live for now until we find our house."

"Will we have a pool?"

"Maybe we will." Luke looked at Missy, "Addy can stay under water longer than the Seals can."

"Wow, that's amazing. How did you learn to do that?"

"I learned in the ocean."

"Do you enjoy the ocean?"

"Yes, I can swim under or float on my back. I can go way out to where I can't see anyone and still find my way back to the shore."

"Lord, that would scare me to death if you did that when I was around. I don't want you to ever do that again. Promise me."

Addy looked at the pretty lady. Was she going to cry again? She sounded like she really cared. "Okay, I promise. Why do you want me to promise you?"

"Because I don't want anything to happen to you. Your daddy will be very sad if something happens to you, and so would I."

"Really."

"Yes, sweetie, really."

23

"Did you have fun with Missy?" Julia asked Addy.

They were all sitting in the backyard talking. Harold was there, as were Ryes, Kane, and Austin. Along with Julia. They had a meeting, and now they had hotdogs in the backyard for lunch.

"Did you meet Missy?" Harold asked Addy.

"Yes, we are good friends. That's what she said, but then she cried."

"Why did she cry?"

"Because she was happy."

"It's probably because of the baby. Mom said it makes women emotional when they are pregnant."

No one said anything. All eyes were on Luke. "Luke, keep calm. She wasn't keeping this from you. She knew you had a lot of things going on. When you told her you had to concern yourself with Addy right now, she decided to wait until you were ready to hear any more news," Julia said. "You are not going to dash over there and yell at her. Because I will stop you. If you saw her, you must not have looked closely, or you would have seen she was pregnant."

Harold looked at each of them. "Were we not supposed to say anything about Missy's baby boy?"

"A boy. Why would she keep this from me."

"Missy didn't keep it from you. Were you listening to me? I already told you she is showing. If you looked at Missy, you would know she's carrying a baby. She isn't hiding anything. She didn't know she was pregnant until two weeks ago. The first person she called was you. And you told her you had to focus on other things. Missy has baby things all around her home. You didn't notice. It's not her fault. So back off, buddy."

"Julia, really, you want to fight me. I'm not blaming Missy for anything. All I'm saying is I saw her yesterday, and she didn't say anything about a baby."

"You weren't the only one there now, were you?"

"Sweetheart, I don't think Luke is upset about anything. Am I right, Luke?"

"Yes, you are right. I'm not upset. I'm a little in shock." He looked around, "Where is Harold?"

"He's probably on his way to Missy's."

"What's wrong. Do I have to go back to Grandma's?"

"No, you will never go back to your grandma. You're my daughter, and you will stay with me always. I'm your father. I love you. I will never let anyone else have you."

"Missy, I'm so sorry. I mentioned your baby boy. I didn't know Luke didn't know about him."

"That's okay, I would have told him already, but he's getting used to having a daughter. You didn't do anything wrong. I'm so glad you are here. I bought a new dresser at an estate sale. I absolutely love it. I tried to get it out, but I didn't want to hurt the baby."

"I'll get it out. Harold, can I talk to Missy alone, please?" it was Luke's voice that came from behind her.

Harold looked at Missy.

"Harold, will you come back later. I wanted someone to stay here tonight with me. I thought I saw someone outside last night."

"I'll be here before dark."

"Thank you."

"What do you mean you thought you saw someone last night. Harold, I'll stay here with Missy."

Missy shook her head. "No, you are not going to. I'll see you later, Harold."

"Why am I not staying here with you?"

"Because you have Addy. She needs you."

"I need you. I want to talk about my son."

"What should I do?" Harold asked.

"Come back and stay here with me. I'm sure it was my imagination. But just one night will calm my nerves."

"Okay, I'll see you later," he said before walking outside.

"Tell me about the baby."

"Well, I took a home test, and it said I wasn't pregnant. But I wasn't feeling good. I was always tired. So when I came back here, I made an appointment. The doctor said I was five months pregnant, and she showed me a picture of the baby. I had her make one for you too," She walked over and opened a door on her desk, and took out the photos of her baby. "This is for you," Missy handed him the picture of the image. "So in about three months, my baby boy will be here."

"Our baby boy."

"Yes, our baby boy. You don't have to worry about me pressuring you for anything. The baby will be here. You can see him anytime you want."

"Missy, I know that. I never thought for a second you

would keep the baby from me. I'm here for you. Why don't you come back to the safe house tonight?"

"Luke, there is no way I'm going to stay at the safe house with you. I listened to what you told me, and I agree with you. Addy needs to know you love her. She needs you right now. You said yourself, Addy never had someone tell her they love her. She has never had a hug. I can take care of the baby and myself. I don't want you to ever worry about us. We will be fine."

"I know you can, but I want to be with you and the baby as well. I don't want to think about you being here where maybe a peeping Tom might be looking in the house while I am safe and secure at the safe house."

"Everything will be fine. I'm going to sell this house. It's not safe for a toddler. He could fall in the water so fast. I'll show you the dresser I got. It goes in the baby's room."

Luke looked around the house, and Julia was right. There were baby things everywhere. He put the dresser in the garage because she wanted to paint it. He walked into the baby's room and looked around. It was perfect, he almost cried.

"You've done a great job here."

"Thank you, Theodore and Harold helped me."

"I'm sorry I wasn't here to help you."

"It's not your job to help me."

"Yes, it is. I'm the baby's father. I want to be here for you and our son. Do you need me to go with you to anything?"

"No, Julia is going with me."

Luke pulled her into his arms. "I want to be with you. I want to be there for my son. I feel like I'm not doing anything for you and the baby. I want to be a big part of his life."

Missy laid her head on his chest and closed her eyes. "I'm always so tired. I swear I could go to sleep right here."

Luke picked her up and carried her to her room. He laid her on the bed and took her shoes off. Then he laid down next to her. He pulled her up next to him and put his hand on her stomach. The baby decided to move around at that time.

Luke stopped, "Was that the baby?"

"Yes, your son is very active. He keeps me awake at night. I think he has his days and nights messed up. That's why I'm selling this house. Can you imagine how fast he could run outside? It scares me just thinking about it."

"Let me buy a house and we can all live together."

"Wait, did you say we can all live together? I don't want to do that. Why would you think I would?"

"I'm sorry, it wasn't right for me to ask that."

"Let's forget about it. I'm going to take a nap. You don't have to stay here. Go home. I don't want Addy to worry about where you are. Luke, please don't feel that you are obligated to do things for me."

"I don't feel obligated. I want to do everything I can for you and the baby. I want to be in on the baby's birth. I want to be in your life. I know you said Julia is going to be there with you but I would also like to be there as well."

"Of course, you can be there. I was going to ask you if you wanted to see the birth of your son. Okay, I'll let you know in advance when I have an appointment, and you can come with me."

HE WAS DRIVING HER CRAZY. Calling her five times a day. Popping in at least three times a day. Missy knew he wanted to be involved in the baby's birth, but it was hard for her to see him all the time and not be with him. She missed them being together. He stayed one night with her when Addy stayed over at Austin's with Ivy. Missy knew Luke missed her

LUKE

as much as she missed him. The last time he was here, he had her up against the wall. Both of them were headed to the bedroom when they heard Addy calling for Luke. Luke stepped back and bent his head, and kissed her again. Then he turned and kissed her tummy.

"Have you thought of a name?"

"I thought I would let you name him. If you want to name him after someone like your dad but can his middle name be Luke. That way, he will know he will always have a piece of you with him."

"I would like that very much. My grandfather's name was James. We can name him James Luke Wilson."

"That sounds perfect to me."

He kissed her again and took another step back. He came so close, telling her right then that he loved her. *What the hell is wrong with me? You can never mutter those words to Missy.*

24

Missy was up at three in the morning peeing when she saw a shadow. She hurried and got her gun and her phone. The first thing she did was call the police, then she called Luke. It rang twice before he answered.

"What's wrong, Sugar?"

"Someone is here in my house."

Luke flew out of bed, pulled his pants on and his boots and ran out to his car. It took ten minutes, the police were there, and Missy was sitting on the step crying. Luke ran to her and pulled her into his arms.

"Luke, I shot that man. I didn't want to, but he broke my bedroom door down."

"It's okay, sweetheart, you did what you had to do. Here, let me hold you."

He pulled her on his lap and held onto her. When he raised his head, he saw Julia walking out of the house.

"The bastard isn't dead. If the cops weren't here, I would have killed him. How are you doing, Missy?"

"Now that I know he's not dead, I feel better. I didn't

want to kill him."

"Who is he?" Luke asked.

"Someone who camped across the river. Apparently, there is a campsite over there where homeless people live. He saw Missy lived alone and was going to rob her."

"Where did I shoot him?"

"You shot him in the groin. Maybe his dick will fall off."

Missy giggled. "I'm going to have a cup of tea. Does anyone else want something?"

"I'll take a cup of coffee," Luke said, walking in behind her. "Are you coming?" he asked, looking at Julia.

"No, Kane is still upset that I ran out of the house without telling him. But when Missy called me, I just wanted to see who she shot."

"Missy, I don't want you staying alone here anymore."

"I know. Jamie will be here in a couple of weeks. My beautiful home was fine when it was just me. But now I have the baby to think of. I'll be moving out starting today."

"Why don't you stay at the safe house?"

"I bought myself a home already. It's not far from here. It has a wrap-around porch a beautiful fenced-in yard. It'll be perfect for a toddler. It also has a fenced-in pool. So Addy will like that when she visits. I'll call the movers and see if they can start today."

"I'm going to see when they can get that guy out of here." Luke walked to Missy's bedroom and saw the guy on the gurney crying.

"I'm going to kill that bitch for shooting me."

Luke grabbed him by the throat and pulled him up. He hissed in the guys ear. "I'm going to kill you before you leave this house. You messed with the wrong woman." Luke slugged him so hard it knocked the guy out cold. Luke would make sure the guy never tried robbing another helpless pregnant woman. He went back into the kitchen and sat down to drink his coffee. He looked at Missy, sitting there drinking her tea while tears ran down her face. He didn't think she even knew she was crying. He stood up and put her on his lap. The baby was kicking like crazy. Luke rubbed her tummy to calm the baby down. He started singing a song to the baby. Missy giggled, as Luke knew she would.

"Where did you learn that song?"

"I wrote it for our baby."

"You wrote it for our baby?"

"Yes, don't you believe me?"

"Yes, I believe you. I'm so happy I'm having a baby with you. You are going to be a wonderful father to Jamie." She kissed him on his forehead.

Luke kissed her on her chin. "Has everyone left?"

"Yes."

He stood her up and took her hand. He walked her to her bathroom where he undressed her and then undressed. He started the shower, and they walked inside.

"I don't know if I want you to see how I look right now."

"I think you are more beautiful than anything in the world. I love your body." Luke looked into her eyes, "Missy Devlin, I love you."

"You love me?"

"Yes, sweetheart, I love you."

"Luke, you don't have to tell me you love me."

"I'm telling you because I do love you. I don't want to keep it to myself any longer."

"Luke, I love you too. I've loved you since the moment I saw you."

"Missy, you couldn't have loved me from the moment you first saw me. I was a dick when I first met you."

"I know. But you can ask anyone we know. I've been telling them I love you from the first moment I saw you.

Umm, that feels good. Missy opened her eyes. Let's go to bed and make love."

"Will it hurt the baby?"

"No, we'll take it easy. Let's use the spare room. My room will need the carpet taken out."

They made love for hours before Luke had to leave. Missy stayed in bed until she heard the movers driving down her driveway. She explained what happened when the man broke into her room. She showed them where she shot him, and they discussed taking the carpet out. She had a carpet guy coming later that day. All four bedrooms were moved and sat up at the new home by the end of the day.

Missy packed most of the kitchen things and put the boxes in her car when Luke and Addy came over. "Hi, you two."

Luke pulled her into his arms and kissed her. He wanted Addy to know he loved Missy, and he wasn't going to hide it. "I hope you haven't been moving these boxes on your own."

"No, I have only moved a couple of them. We should put some boxes in your truck, and you can follow me home."

"I'll move the boxes. You can tell me which ones you want me to load."

25

Luke walked to where Ash stood, talking to a man they were flying out to North Dakota. His son had been kidnapped, and his wife was in the hospital with three gunshot wounds, and the Nanny was dead. They didn't know if she would make it or not. The kidnappers demanded two million dollars to get his son back. They could hear the three-year-old crying in the background when the kidnapper made their demand.

Luke looked at the man. His name was Rick Herrod. He was a billionaire, and he was told not to get the FBI involved. He called his buddy, Shane McKenna, and Shane told him to call the Band of Navy Seals. "Listen to me. We aren't going to take any chances with your son's life. We do this the way I say. I've dealt with kidnappers before, so I know how their minds work. They will be skittish, and that's not good. The first thing we do is listen to the background noise to see if we can hear anything to give us an idea of where they are."

"I just want my son. If they want more money, they can have it. I'll give them everything I have. Please get my son. He must be so scared." Rick put his hands over his face and cried.

Luke couldn't imagine how scared these parents were. "Let's go to where he's going to meet you. Now, listen, it's dark. They won't be able to tell I'm not you. We are the same build and height. When you see them walk toward me, you can't say anything. We can't blow this. We'll only get this one chance. Let's go."

They drove for fifteen miles before Luke pulled over and let Ash and Steven out. "Rick, please listen to Ash."

"You don't have to worry about me. I'm not going to do anything and risk my son's life. I'll be with Ash, and I won't say a word."

Luke drove slowly around the area and then headed for the meet-up spot. He knew Ash and Rick would be right behind him. In case something went wrong. He got the bag out of the back seat and walked to the first table where the note said to go.

"Leave the bag and walk back to your car."

"Where is my son?"

"Your son is safe. You need to get the hell away from here before we kill him."

"The deal was that I give you the money, and you give me my son."

"I know what the deal was. But I'm changing it."

"No, you are sticking to the deal we made. I want my son. You are not getting this money until I get my son."

"I'm the one who makes the rules. Now I want more money."

"Give me my son."

"I have the gun. I can shoot you right here and take the money."

"You can try to take the money." Luke pulled his gun out of its holster, "Oh look, I have a gun as well. I wonder who's the best shot. "Give me my son, or I will blow your fucking head off."

"Shit, you're crazy. Calm down. I'll give you your son. I had to give him something to put him to sleep. He wouldn't stop crying."

Luke prayed Ash could keep Rick quiet. The guy walked to the back of his vehicle, and Luke saw him pick something up. It wasn't the boy. It was another gun. Shit. I'm going to have to shoot him. As soon as the guy stood up, Luke shot the gun out of his hand.

"Don't fuck with me. I want my son, or I will blow you away."

"Ethel, bring the kid out here." A woman walked out of the bushes carrying the boy.

Luke never took his eyes off the man. He walked over and stood next to the table. "Put my son down softly. He better not be harmed, or I'm going to kill you."

"He's just sleeping, as I said. Give me the money."

"The money is on the table. You can get it after I take my son. Both of you back up."

"We want the money first."

"I don't give a fuck what you want. Move!"

Both of them backed up. Luke didn't take the gun off of the man. He walked over and looked at the boy. He looked like he was sleeping. "What did you give him?"

"Some gummy bear melatonin. The kid wouldn't shut up. I had to give him something. He thought he was eating candy. Now, give me the money."

"Stay where you are." Luke bent and picked up the boy. He put him over his shoulder, and Ash walked out from behind a tree. His gun trained on both of them. Rick walked over and took his son from Luke. Then he walked back to the vehicle. They stood there with their guns on the two kidnappers.

"You tricked me. I told you not to bring anyone else. Now I'm going to have to kill your entire family."

"Did you get all of that, Emma?"

"Yep, I got everything. Emma Stone, Special Agent FBI, walked from behind the trees along with four other FBI agents.

Luke turned to leave when something struck him in his back that took him to his knees. They all turned as another woman got out of the vehicle. Emma turned and shot her. The woman landed on the ground dead.

"You killed my sister," the other lady shouted.

"Arrest these people and read them their rights. I don't want any of them being released. I want them to spend a long time in prison."

Ash ran to Luke. He wasn't breathing. He turned him over and ripped his shirt open. "Damn, I didn't think she shot him with a gun."

"It wasn't a gun," said the man who kidnapped the boy. "It shoots hard projectiles. It must have hit him where his heart was. It stopped his heart from beating."

"What was it!" Ash shouted. He worked on Luke as he talked. "Call an ambulance."

Rick Herrod walked up to them carrying his son. He handed him to Emma and bent down to see what happened to Luke. He turned him over and pounded on his chest. After about five hits to Luke's chest, he started back breathing, and his heart started pumping. But he was still unconscious.

"Why won't he wake up?"

"He will. Let's go to the hospital. I need to see my wife and to let her know we have our son."

The ambulance with Luke in it left for the hospital, and Ash followed behind it. When they got to the hospital, Ash went with Luke. He explained to the doctor what happened.

The doctor turned Luke over, and there was a hole where the projectile hit him.

"Damn, it broke the skin. Here it is." He took a small tool and dug into Luke's back. Out popped a hard black object shaped like a cone. The doctor put it in a plastic bag and handed it to his nurse. "Don't lose that. I'll give it to the FBI."

The doctor looked at Luke. "I've never seen anything like this before. I hope to hell there are no more of these guns out there."

Ash watched Luke seeing if he was going to wake up. "Yeah, I've seen a lot of weapons but none like this. It must be homemade. The FBI has the gun. When do you think Luke will wake up?"

"I don't know. That's something I can't tell you. I'm going to send him for an MRI; hopefully, nothing else was damaged. You might as well go to the waiting room. I'll let you know when he's out."

"Okay, I'll make a couple of phone calls. Be sure you call me when you know something." Ash raised his head up, and Emma watched him from the nurse station. He shook his head. "They don't know anything yet. Did you get that black thing that was in his back?"

"Yes, what the hell is going on in this world when people start making their own bullets."

Ash shook his head. "They are giving him an MRI right now. I hope he wakes up soon because I don't want to call Missy and tell her what happened."

"So they are finally a couple. It's about damn time. Jeez, what took so long anyway. I told Missy to tell him two years ago that she loved him but she wanted to wait for him to realize he loved her first. So I guess he finally realized it."

"Yeah, he did. They have a baby that's due any day. Luke wasn't supposed to be here, but when we got a look at the dad, we knew Luke was the best match for him."

"Hey, I have to get back home. I miss my babies and my husband. Call me when you find out what's going on with Luke. I bet his back is going to be hurting for a long time."

"I'm sure it will. I guess I'll be seeing you around."

"I'm going to retire from the FBI. I want to be with my family. Liam's going to be happy when I tell him. You take care, Ash, and tell Willow I said hello."

"I'll tell her. Congratulations on your retirement."

"Thank you."

Ash decided to find out where Rick's wife was. He wanted to see how his son was doing. When he walked into the room, he could hear Rick talking to his wife. Ash smiled. It sounded like Rick's wife was going to make it. "Hello."

"Ash, I want to introduce you to my wife. Shannon, this is Ash Beckham. He was one of the men who saved our son."

"Ash, how can I thank you?" She started to cry.

"I'm just happy to see you and Little Ricky alive. I can see he woke up. I only wanted to check-in to see how you all were doing."

"How is Luke?" Rick asked.

"They took him in for an MRI. You should have seen what they took out of his back. Hopefully, he'll wake up as your son did, and everyone will be happy."

"Please keep me informed on how Luke is doing. We'll pray for him."

26

"Damn, my back is killing me. I wish you would have taken a picture of that damn thing that went into my back and stopped my heart. I'm so happy to be going home. Addy is probably worried she will have to go back to her grandma. The damn woman who was angry because Addy didn't drown."

"What about Missy. Are you worried that she will be worried that you don't love her anymore?"

"No, I'm not concerned about Missy. She knows how much I love her. She told me she's loved me since the first time she met me."

"Yeah, she has. We all knew that because Missy has been telling us for years how much she loves you. All of us tried telling her that you would never love her because of Susan. I'm glad we were wrong."

"Yeah, me too. So, everyone knew Missy loved me?"

"Yep, all of us."

"How come no one told me?"

"It wasn't up to us to tell you. It was between you and Missy."

"Yes, Missy and me. Who would ever know how great my life has turned out."

"So when is the wedding?"

"There isn't going to be a wedding."

"What do you mean?"

"I'm not ever getting married again. Everyone knows how I feel about marriage."

"Yes, but that was with Susan. Missy isn't anything like Susan. I'm not going to advise you on what to do, but don't you think Missy deserves more than just your body."

"She has more than my body. Missy has all of me, forever. You were right. I don't want your advice. Maybe one day we'll be married, just not right now."

"Who's watching your daughter while you are working?"

"I hired a nanny to be with her while I'm not home. We rented a small apartment, until I can find a home to buy."

"Hmmm."

"What's that for?"

"I feel like you are using Missy."

"Damn it, Ash, please stay out of my life."

"Did you think to ask Missy if Addy could stay with her?"

"I thought about it. I didn't want to impose, plus I didn't want Missy to get the wrong idea."

"So you don't really love her enough to ask her to watch your daughter because you don't want her to get the wrong idea."

"Okay, I admit that sounds horrible. I do love Missy more than anything. I don't know why it scares me to think about getting married. I must be crazy. I want to spend every minute with Missy. Of course, I do. I'm sure she's hurting because of the way I've handled this. I need to talk to her."

"What do you mean she's gone. Where is she?"

"I don't know where she is. Missy comes and goes as she pleases. She doesn't have to tell anyone where she goes. Maybe she said something to Riley. She didn't tell me she was going out of town."

"Okay, thanks, Julia. I'll call Harold and see if she said something to him. The baby is due tomorrow."

"Good luck in finding her. I'm sure she's around here somewhere. I believe her feelings were hurt when you didn't trust her enough to leave Addy with her. She never said that her feelings were hurt, just a feeling I have I suppose; women instincts and all."

"Yeah, I'm thinking I screwed up on other things as well."

"At least you're recognizing them now. Goodbye, Luke."

"Bye."

Luke was really worried, it'd been three weeks, and he hadn't heard from Missy. The baby must have already been born. *No one is taking this as a serious matter about her not coming home. Where the hell is she? Stop and think about the last conversation you had with her. She wanted to know if she could bring Addy to her house. What were the exact words I said to her? I told her that Addy was fine where she was because the Nanny had experience with kids. Why the hell would I tell her something like that? What did she say to me? She said, okay, I thought it would be nice to have her here. I'm a fucking dick.*

27

"You are so beautiful. I love you, sweetheart. We'll let you visit your daddy when we go home."

"Missy, when are you going back to Montana?"

"I'm not sure yet. I'm going to call Luke and let him know the baby and I are fine. That he doesn't have to worry about us. I mean, he didn't let Addy stay with me because I wasn't experienced enough to watch a seven-year-old. What if he thought I couldn't watch my baby. What if he hired a Nanny to take care of the baby and I had no say."

"He says he loves me, but he doesn't want to be with me. He has no say on where I go or what I do. I was so angry when he rented that apartment, knowing I bought a five-bedroom home. He was afraid to become closer to me. Because he has said that we will never marry. Luke thought I would pressure him to marry me. He told me once he wanted us to live together, but then he rented an apartment. That hurt. But I wasn't going to let it bother me. Then he said that about me watching his daughter and it was the final straw."

"I don't know what to say. Tell Luke how you feel. He knows you love him. I'm sure he is pulling his hair out, wondering where you are."

"Dakota, I left him messages. Believe me, when I went into labor here, I was shocked. I was only going to be here one night. Then when I got off the plane, my water broke. I was taken by ambulance to the hospital. I was scared to death. But it wasn't as bad as I thought it would be."

"I'm sorry you were alone. I was in shock when I saw you carrying this baby. You have to call Julia or Polly.."

"Okay, I will. I promise."

"Have you talked to Marc lately?"

"No, not lately. Why?"

"No reason. I just haven't seen much of him."

"He has a baby boy he's bringing up on his own. The mother, Kathy, passed away from cancer when Adam, the baby, was one month old. They weren't together, Kathy was gay, but she wanted a child. She said she saw Marc and decided he would be perfect for her baby. I knew her from my cabin in North Carolina. When she told me she was dying, I got a hold of Marc, and he took care of her until she died. He's had Adam since he was born."

"Oh my goodness, that's so sad. Isn't it just like Marc to do something like that?"

"Yes, it is. I told Kathy that Marc would help her. Are you staying in Nashville?"

"No, I have to leave today. I'm meeting Skye in Hawaii. She's rented a home on the beach for a month there."

"That sounds like fun."

"I'm sure it will be. Did I tell you that Skye is retiring from the FBI?"

"That's wonderful news. I bet her kids are happy. What about Lucas? Is he staying with the DEA?"

"Until the end of the year, then he's retiring. They bought

a large RV, and they are taking trips across the country. Skye said she would record each trip so the kids would have something to watch when they were older."

"I've always wanted to buy one of those. I mean, that would be perfect. You could be driving around in your own home. If the baby is hungry, all you have to do is pull over and feed the baby. What a great idea. You can pull into one of those cute parks and hook up for the night. You could even stay longer if you want to."

"Missy, you'll let me know if you buy an RV, won't you?"

"Why would you want to know if I buy an RV?"

"So people will know where you are. You tend to disappear and forget to call and let the people who love you know where you are."

"I said I was going to call Luke. I did leave him a few messages. He needs to check them once in a while."

"What about Polly?"

"I'll call her too."

"Okay, I have to leave. Congratulations on this beautiful baby girl. I thought you were having a boy."

"I thought so too. Jami was a surprise, but she was a beautiful surprise. I will have to change a lot of things like the colors in her room. I also have to buy little girl clothes. I'm glad most of the baby clothes are white or yellow. I won't have to go shopping for a while."

"If you do buy an RV, please drive carefully."

"I'm only going to look at them."

"Okay. I will see you when you come back to California for a visit."

Missy loved her RV. It had three pop-outs. Missy called it her home away from home. She was driving it back to

Montana. She called Julia and told her where she was. She asked her to contact Luke and tell him she and the baby would be home soon.

"Missy, I can't believe you took off without telling anyone. We've all been so worried about you. Why haven't you answered your phone?"

"If you must know, I didn't want to talk to Luke. He said I didn't have the experience to take care of his daughter. I was afraid he would hire someone to take care of my baby. You know how he can be?"

"Yes, but you two love each other."

"I don't care. If he can't trust me to watch his daughter, I don't want to be with him."

"He was shot in the back. He's going to be okay. He still has a hard time catching his breath, and he's scared to death something happened to you and the baby. He actually died when he was shot. Their client brought him back to life by pounding on his chest and making his heart start back up."

"What? Oh my Lord, I'll call him tomorrow. I have called him four times and left messages. I can't help it if he hasn't checked his voice mail. Thank the lord he's alright. I miss him so much. But I can't be with someone who doesn't trust me to take care of his child."

"That pisses me off. I don't blame you. If you've left him messages, then that's all he needs. Tell me about your baby boy."

Missy giggled and took a picture of Jami with the pink ribbon in her hair. She sent it to Julia.

"You had a girl. Oh, Missy, she's beautiful. I can't wait to hold her. Where did you take the picture?"

"In my RV, it's like driving around in a house."

"You be careful."

"I will. I'll see you in a few days. I have to get Sheriff from the kennel."

LUKE

"Luke has Sheriff."

"How did he get Sheriff?"

"She ran away from the kennel, and they called him."

Missy sighed. *I'm tired there are always so many things going on to keep me busy..* "Bye, Julia."

∼

"WHAT DO you mean she called me? I didn't get a phone call from Missy."

"Check your voicemail. Missy was pretty hurt that you didn't trust her to watch Addy. She said you might want to hire someone to watch Jami." Julia didn't say Jami was a girl.

"I was wrong in saying that. But I didn't mean it to sound that way. I told her that because the baby was almost here and she would be doing too much. I didn't mean it to sound like I didn't trust her." Luke was talking while going through his phone. "Oh fuck, she did call me. How could I have missed these calls? She called me this morning also." He dialed Missy's number, and it went to voice mail. "She's not answering."

"She's driving. And if she sees the calls from you, she probably doesn't want to talk to you while she's driving."

"She's driving. Where was she?"

"Nashville."

"She's driving with the baby from Nashville." He was looking through his phone. It said he had photos to look at. He clicked it open, and there were pictures of his baby. At least ten images when the baby was born. Luke wiped his eyes. His baby was perfect.

"She bought herself an RV. She says it's like driving a house down the road. At night she stays in RV parks. She is taking it slow because she just had a baby. Missy didn't plan on having the baby in Nashville. She went to finalize the sale of her home there, and she went into labor when she got off the plane two weeks early."

"She's driving an RV, all alone."

"No, she has Jami with her."

"Did she say what day she'll be back?"

"She'll be here tomorrow. If I was you, I would be thinking of a spectacular apology."

"Yep. Thanks, Julia. I better go pick Addy up from school."

"Luke, women don't like to be told they aren't capable of watching a child. That would be one of the top worst things you could ever say to her."

28

Missy drove down her road and saw Luke's vehicle parked out front. He was sitting on the front porch. She slowed down and came to a complete stop. Luke stood up and walked to her door. Missy couldn't help the tears that fell from her eyes. These last few weeks have been hard. And then she heard he was shot in the back.

"Hey, Sugar, are you going to open your door?"

She opened her door, and he took her by the waist and lifted her out. He held her in his arms as she cried. "I'm so sorry. I didn't mean that I didn't trust you to take care of Addy. I meant I didn't want you to have to take care of Addy when our baby would be here in a few weeks. I love you so much. I would never hurt you. Please say you believe me."

Missy sniffed. "I believe you. I'm sorry I went out of town. I was only going to be gone one night and then I went into labor. I was so scared. I don't want to have our other children without you there with me."

"I will always be with you. I love you so much. Missy Devlin, will you marry me. I want to spend every night with you, in bed next to me. I want to be with you and only you always."

"Yes, I'll marry you. Let's get married soon." That's when they heard the baby waking up. Missy went around to the door and opened it.

Luke followed her to where the baby was strapped into a car seat. "He's beautiful."

"Look again," Missy said, smiling.

Luke got a massive smile on his face when he saw the pink bow on his daughter's head. Her hair was as red as her mommy's and just as curly. "She's beautiful. What did we name her?" a tear fell from his eye.

"Her name is Jami, after her grandpa. Her middle name is Mae after my grandma."

"Jami... Thank you for this precious gift. Can I hold her?"

"I know she would love that. I swear I'm so glad to be home with my family. Where is Addy?

"She's in the backyard playing on the trampoline."

"I was hoping she would like that. She's going to be surprised to see she has a sister instead of a brother. Let's go tell her."

Luke held the baby in his arms with his other arm around Missy. He bent his head and kissed his daughter, then he kissed the top of Missy's head.

"Your house will be full of women. We better try for a boy next time. Julia said you were injured. I'm so sorry I wasn't here to take care of you."

"Sugar, you didn't have time to take care of me. I'm almost completely healed. I'm still a little sore. But I'll let you kiss me all better."

"Oh, you know I will. Are you and Addy moving in here with Jami and me?"

"Nothing could keep me from staying with you and my beautiful daughter." Luke smiled when he saw his other daughter doing flips on the trampoline. "Addy, look who's here."

Addy looked up and smiled. She ran over, and Missy picked her up and hugged her. "I missed you so much, Addy."

"You missed me. I missed you too. Can I see the baby?"

"Yes, you can. Let's sit over here." They all sat on the patio sofa with Luke in the middle.

"Is this my little brother? I don't think you should give him a pink bow."

Both Luke and Missy burst into laughter. "The doctor was wrong. We had a baby girl instead of a boy. Maybe our next one will be a boy."

"So, I have a little sister. I can teach her everything I know. I'll tell her she can't jump into the pool with just her panties, or Daddy will get angry. He said I had to wear a swimsuit. I will tell her she can climb in bed with me whenever she wants to. She will never have to sleep outside by herself with the dogs. We will always tell her we love her and give her a lot of kisses and hugs. Thank you for giving me, my sister."

"Addy, you will be the best sister any baby has ever had. I'm so happy you are my little girl."

"I'm so happy you are my mommy, and my daddy is my daddy. I don't want to visit my grandma ever, she doesn't love me."

Luke held her on one side and Jami on the other. "You have us now. We will never let you visit your grandma or your uncle. I love you so much, Addy."

"I love you too, Daddy. I love Mommy and Jami too." She looked at Missy, "Why did you give my sister a boy's name?"

Missy laughed and wrapped her arms around all three of them. "I'm so lucky I have you three in my life. The three loves of my life."

Luke kissed her. "I'm the lucky one."

Addy shook her head. "I'm the lucky one. I don't have to live with my grandma anymore."

Luke chuckled. "We are all blessed."

THE END

THE END

Dear reader.

Thank you, for your continued support. I really appreciate that you read my books.

If you can please leave me a review for this book, I would appreciate it enormously.

Your reviews allow me to get validation I need to keek going as an Indie author.

Just a moment of your time is all that is needed. I will try my best to give you the

best books I can write

RYES

My Book

KEEP READING FOR MORE OF THE BAND OF NAVY SEALS

PLEASE FOLLOW ME ON BOOKBUB

https://www.bookbub.com/profile/susie-mciver

https://www.goodreads.com/author/dashboard

RYES

When Ryes Cohen opened his bedroom door, and his wife was riding the neighbor's seventeen-year-old son, like she was on a bucking bull, he felt like dancing a jig. He knew that was the best thing that could have happened to him. That's why he laughed when he saw them in bed together. If Sandra had a gun, he would have been dead. She was so mad that she got caught.

Ryes's wife refused to divorce him. Because she wanted his father's money when he died. Ryes told her his dad was as healthy as a forty-year-old man. Sandra refused to listen to him. So he snapped a few photos of her and the kid and went to find his lawyer. He never really loved his wife. She was a conniving bitch who tricked him into getting married. She told him she was pregnant. There was no way he would let her raise his child. Then she refused to divorce him.

He should have listened to his dad when he said to talk to her doctor. Sandra was beautiful on the outside. On the inside, she was pure evil. Ryes only noticed the outside when she tricked him. That's when her true self came out. His lieutenant had called him the week before about joining their Band of Navy Seals security team. So he filed for a divorce, told the neighbor that he caught his son in bed with his wife, packed everything he wanted that belonged to him, and made his way to California.

He would leave it to his lawyer to get Sandra out of his house. That house belonged to his grandfather. He built it for his wife when they married seventy-five years ago. Ryes would make sure Sandra got out of there if he had to burn the house down. He didn't have to do that. His lawyer threatened to show the photos to his wife's parents. She signed the papers and moved out. Ryes let his cousin live there while he wasn't there.

That was six years ago. He loved working with his Navy Seal buddies. Now he lived in Montana, at the safe house. The business was run by a super cute twenty-seven-year-old who looked like she should still be in high school. Riley Kaiser made his blood boil when they stood next to each other. She ran everything, and with her in charge, the business ran smoothly for the team. She was the kindest and funniest woman he knew. When the cartel was after her DEA father, they almost killed Riley, and she's been with them since that time. She took over the business operation, and Ryes didn't think they could get along without her.

Ryes had strong feelings for Riley, but when he asked Austin if he should ask her out, Austin told him to keep the hell away from her. Riley was too important to the team. He said for him to screw it up. Ryes didn't think he would screw anything up, but what if he did. Who would take care of them? So he never acted on his feelings, and they were getting stronger every year.

Riley watched Ryes as he pulled himself out of the pool. Damn, he was hot. She would give anything if he would walk in and pull her into his arms and carry her off to his room. Not that she knew much of anything about making love. The things she knew she could write on a post-it. She did read romance novels. She loved to read romance books. She bent her head and pretended to be watering her herb garden. She knew if Ryes saw her face, he would see how much she wanted him to take her right there on the grass. She shook her head at the direction of her thoughts were going. She needed to go on a diet if she was thinking that way. Some people would say she had an hourglass figure. She would say she's overweight.

Maybe the next time Ryan Grant asked her out, she would say yes. He worked for them he put security cameras in all of their safe homes, among other things. Riley knew there were many things Ryan was good at. He was an Army Ranger Special Forces guy. He looked like Clark Kent with his black-rimmed glasses and his striking blue eyes. Yep if he asked her, she would go out with him. She was sure he could teach her something about sex and other things she needed to know before she asked Ryes out on a date. Riley giggled, thinking about how shocked Ryes was going to be when she asked him out. First, she needed more experience with men. The women Ryes went with didn't look like Riley.

"What's so funny, sweet Riley?"

Riley turned her head. She didn't know Ryes stood so close to her, with only his swimming trunks and that beautiful bare chest that was solid muscles. It would be so easy to just reach out and touch him. "Nothing, I was just remembering something from when I was young."

"Want to share it with me? I could use a good laugh."

"No, it's kind of private."

"Either it is private, or it's not. There isn't something that is kind of private. Is it a secret?"

Riley looked up at him. He had the prettiest blue-gray eyes. His wet hair hung in his eyes. Before she knew it, her fingers reached up and moved his bangs out of his eyes. Then she noticed his eyes darken. And he bent his head. Riley just knew he was going to kiss her when Kane walked outside and messed it up. Riley looked over at Kane and frowned.

"What's up?"

"Nothing. What's up with you?" Riley said. She heard Ryes chuckle. Was he laughing at her?

"I mean, what do you have for me? You called me over here."

"Oh, sorry. Do you remember when I told you both about the woman who said she was being followed? Well, she called this morning and said she was still being followed. She's pretty scared. I told her you guys would be there with her until we find out who is following her. She lives in Texas. This is her file. Good luck." Riley picked some herbs and walked back inside. She inhaled the scent of the herbs and smiled. She loved her garden

"Thanks. See you when we get back, Riley. Ryes almost kissed her. It's a good thing Kane came out when he did. Or Ryes was pretty sure he would have carried her off to his room. Damn, those beautiful eyes of hers were hypnotizing him."

"Were you about to kiss Riley?"

"Yeah, I'm glad you came out when you did. I've had this thing for Riley for a few years. I'm relieved I didn't blow it."

"Why don't you ask her out? Didn't you see the frown she gave me for interrupting you?"

"No, I was too busy frowning at you myself. Austin thought it would mess everything up, and we would lose Riley as our boss lady. If it didn't work out," They called her their boss because she told all of them what to do, and where to go.

"Wait, are you telling me you asked Austin if you should ask Riley out?"

"Yeah, I mentioned it to him a few years ago."

"A few years ago. Ask Riley before someone else does. I heard Ryan asked her out. Don't listen to Austin. He's afraid he'll get stuck with doing her job."

"Damn, it. You're right. I was so fucking stupid. I feel like punching Austin. So Ryan asked her out. Ryan is never around. If he asked her out, then I damn sure can." Ryes thought back to the first time he met Riley. Kane had saved her from the cartel. She was so sick. Her hair was blue. She was freezing. She had been kidnapped and taken to a cabin in the woods. When she looked at him with those beautiful eyes of hers, something inside felt like it shifted to the right place in his body. He remembered it was snowing. Kane killed the guy, but others were coming for her. She had been sick for a long time. But when her parents went into hiding because her dad was DEA and the cartel was after him. She blossomed with the team taking care of her. Everyone loved Riley. She cooked for them and took care of everyone there.

Ryes loved her differently than the others did. He didn't really know what he felt for her. He just knew it was powerful.

"Hey Ryan, can I talk to you?"

"Sure you can. What's on your mind?"

"Do you remember when you asked me out?"

"Yes, and you broke my heart."

Riley giggled. "I didn't break your heart. Anyway, I think I want to go out to dinner with you. Maybe a movie. What do you think?"

"I say when are we going?"

"Well, since I know your schedule. I say we go out tonight."

"I would be honored to take you to dinner."

"Great, I'll meet you here in the kitchen at six." Riley smiled. "Okay. You should know I don't date much. What I'm saying is, I don't have a lot of experience. So I wondered if I could ask you a few questions about dating stuff while we are on our date. Also, I know I'm overweight. Does it turn men off if a woman is overweight like I am?"

"What kind of stuff? You're not overweight, so don't think about losing weight and going on a diet. You're curvy. Men love curvy women. Now, what questions were you talking about?"

"About dating?"

"Riley, have you had anyone talk to you about the birds and bees? I mean, has your mom had that talk with you?"

Riley felt her face burning. "I know about the birds and bees. It's just that I've only been on a few dates, so I want to make sure I do everything right for when I have another date. I know that sounds crazy, and I'm sorry, but I need to learn more about what I am supposed to do on a date. I mean, how far am I supposed to go on a first date?"

"Okay, so let me get this straight. You want me to teach you about dating. What you should do and what not to do?"

"Yes."

2

"Riley, honey, all you have to do is be yourself. Everyone loves you. You have a beautiful personality. So just be yourself."

"What about making love. I've only done that once, and it was nothing special like in the books. In fact, it was painful and a bit yucky."

"I am not going to teach you about making love. When you find someone you want to have sex with, then everything will fall into place."

Riley rolled her eyes. "Oh, brother. I have already found the one I want to have sex with. He hasn't asked me out, so I'm going to ask him out as soon as he gets back here. But I first need to learn a few things."

Ryan sighed. *Was he going to have to tell Riley how it's supposed to be done?* "Let's go sit down," he took her hand and guided her over to the sofa, "the way it goes is you let the man ask you out. If you are thinking about having sex with this guy, you wait until the moment is right. When the time is right, you will know. You can't plan all of it ahead of time."

"So you aren't going to help me."

"Don't ask anyone else. We'll go to dinner tonight, and we'll talk tonight about what you should know. I'll pick you up in the kitchen at six."

Riley smiled. "Okay, I better get back to work. I'll see you at six."

Ryan was a nervous wreck. What the hell was he supposed to do? He picked up his jacket and walked to the front door, then he turned and headed to Riley's office. "Riley, I have to run an errand. I'll be right back."

"Okay."

"He headed to Elie's. Someone had to talk to Riley. Would it embarrass her if he got someone else involved? He knew it would, so instead, he went to the flower shop and then Julia's bakery. He bought an assortment of flowers and some cupcakes. When he got back to the safe house, he walked into Riley's kitchen, as they called it, and gave her the flowers and the cupcakes.

"You bought these for me."

"Sure, do you like them?"

"I love them. I'm going to keep these beautiful flowers right here on the table. Thank you."

"You're welcome. I also got us some cupcakes."

"Yummy. I wonder if Austin made them."

"I think he must have. I had one of the lemon ones, and it was delicious. Where do you want to go for dinner?"

"There is an excellent Mexican restaurant out of town. Have you tried it?"

"Yes, you're right, it has great food. We'll go there. You don't mind if I take the phone, do you? I don't have anyone else to answer it."

"Do you work every day?"

"I do. I don't mind. Because I'm here anyway."

"They need to get someone to help you so you can do whatever you want. I'm sure you want a day off once in a while. Who would be here if you took time off?"

"I guess one of the guys would do it. Austin taught me everything. So maybe he would do it. I think if I wanted to take time off of work, then I would just do it."

"Well, that's good to know. I was worrying for nothing. Haven't you been to see your parents?"

"Yes, I went a couple of years ago. It was kind of strange. My mom looked like I was about to bring the cartel down on their heads, so now all I do is zoom call them. Why were you worried about me?" Riley studied Ryan for a moment. *He bought me flowers and cupcakes. He's worried about me working and not having a day off. I hope he doesn't think I want to practice how to make love with him.* "You know Ryan, I've been thinking that I would talk to my mom about dating and the other stuff I wanted to know about. So we don't have to go to dinner tonight."

"Well, why don't we go as friends?"

"Okay, I would like that." *As long as I don't have to get naked, I'm fine.*

29

Ryes looked at Kane. "I haven't seen any sign of anyone following this woman. Do you think maybe she wanted some company and thought since she had to pay us, we could stay with her as long as she kept paying us?"

"I've been thinking the same thing. It's been a week, and we've seen no sign of anyone following her. I mean, she invites women friends over every day. Is that to show them she has bodyguards? We'll talk to her at dinner tonight and tell her we think the guy has stopped following her. Hang on." Ryes stopped talking and jumped out of his seat. He ran into the backyard and grabbed the collar of a young man who was looking in the window.

"What the hell are you doing here? And why have you been following Miss White?" Ryes demanded. The guy wouldn't say anything. Ryes pushed him in a chair.

"I'll be damn, there was someone following her," Kane said, leaning against the wall. "Did you check him for weapons?"

"I don't have any weapons. I only wanted to meet Daphine White."

"Why did you want to meet her?"

"Because she gave me away when I was born. I wanted to see why she gave me away."

"I didn't give you away. I've never had a child. I'm only a few years older than you are."

Both Ryes and Kane rolled their eyes over that lie. "Where did you get your information from?" Ryes asked.

The adoption house gave it to me." He pulled a piece of paper out of his pocket. "It says Daphine Elaine White gave a newborn boy up for adoption. That was twenty years ago."

Daphine sat down. Ryes could see she was shaking. "Do you have anything to say?"

Elaine was my identical twin sister. Both of us were named Daphine. Elaine went by her middle name. My middle name is Anne. I haven't seen Elaine since she was eighteen. Our parents hunted for her for years before they gave up, assuming she was dead. She ran away with this guy who was in a motorcycle gang. My parents hated him. To be honest, they hated everyone we wanted to date. Elaine was the brave one she ran away. She looked at the young man."

"What's your name?"

"Jackson."

"Jackson. I wish I knew where my sister was, but I haven't seen her since she turned eighteen."

He nodded his head and stood. "I won't bother you again." He turned around and left.

The three in the living room sat there for a minute. Before Ryes looked at Daphine. "Why did you lie to him?"

"I don't want him to ever know the truth about his birth."

"Do you want to tell us about it?"

"Why would I want to tell you anything about that time in

my life?" With no thought to what she was doing, she began to tell them about that time in her life. "My sister did run away with a man. She ran away with my husband. I was so hurt. I did stupid things. I started going to the clubs drinking. Most of the time, I can't remember how I got home. Sometimes I would wake up in bed with men I didn't know. When I became pregnant, I moved away. I had my child then I moved back home. The adoption house wasn't supposed to give my name out to anyone. I'm going to sue them."

"So you don't want to get to know him. He's your family."

"He's someone I gave birth to. He's not my family."

Ryes saw her wipe a tear away. "So I guess it was your son who was following you. He was trying to get the courage to talk to you."

"My parents up and left when I told them I was pregnant. They said we are washing our hands of you and your sister. We felt terrible for you because Anne ran away with your husband. But then you had to embarrass your father and me by going out every night and getting pregnant. So I lost my family because of some circumstances that happened because of me. My sister's name is Anne."

The doorbell went off, and Ryes opened the door. "Hello."

"I must have dropped my keys."

"Come in."

Daphine, Jackson dropped his keys." Everyone started looking around for keys. They were found outside. Before Jackson could leave, Daphine started to cry. "Is she alright?" Jackson asked looking at Ryes.

Ryes shrugged his shoulders. "I don't know. I hope so. Are you okay, Daphine?"

"No, sit down."

"Who?"

"All three of you." Ryes ignored her, as did Kane. Jackson

sat on the sofa. "I lied to you. Anne did run away with a man. He was my husband. I went a little crazy at that time. And went out almost every night. I don't know who all I went out with. I shamed my parents, and I hadn't seen them since I told them I was pregnant. They up and left; I haven't heard from them since that day. I don't even know if they are still alive. I gave birth to you. I thought of you every day. The best thing I did was let someone else raise you. I was in bad shape back then. I'm not doing much better right now. I'm sorry I lied to you. Did you want to ask me any questions?"

"I know where my grandparents are. I also know where your sister is. Your husband stayed with her a year, then he ran off with her friend. She isn't doing well. She's hooked on drugs. I also know where my father is. I knew when you were telling me all that stuff before wasn't true."

"You did?"

"Yeah."

"Why do you want to find me? I'm not anything special."

"I just wanted to meet you."

"Can you tell me about yourself?"

"My parents couldn't have kids, so they adopted me. They were great parents. They died a few years ago in an accident. I would have never tried looking for you if they were alive. I'm a Marine. I joined when I got out of college. I'm going overseas, and I just wanted to meet you."

Daphine wiped at her eyes. I wish I could change things, but I can't. Every year your family sends me pictures of you. I went looking for you three months after I gave you up for adoption. I had rights, so I could have gotten you back. Your parents loved you. Your father cried when I showed up. Your mother fainted. We visited for hours all of us cried. They promised me they would send me pictures. I'm sorry they are gone. You had the best people you could have had to raise you. They were so much better than me."

"Thank you for telling me this. When my parents died, I went through all of their papers. I saw the letters you wrote to them. I knew they were sending you photos of me. I wanted to see if maybe we could write to each other while I'm away?"

"Did you say you want to write to me? I would love to write to you."

"Also, your parents are not decent people. I met them. You're lucky they are out of your life."

"Thank you! Can you stay for dinner?"

"I wish I could, but we ship out at midnight."

"Please be careful."

"I will." Both of them stood up, "Can I hug you goodbye?"

"Yes, I would like that."

Kane stood there as Daphine cried. She has cried since Jackson left. He looked at his watch. "Well, that ended well." He heard Ryes laughed from the kitchen. He noticed Ryes got the hell out of there when Kane handed her the entire box of Kleenexes.

"Can you believe my son wants me to write him? I think I'm going to start a letter right now."

Ryes looked at Daphine. "So I guess we're through."

"Thank you both so much. I would never have the courage to talk to Jackson without you two being here. Are you staying the night?"

"No, I think we'll get our things and leave. I'm glad everything turned out well for you and Jackson. Riley will send you some forms."

"Is that her name? What a cute name. She is so pleasant to talk with. Thank you for everything."

MORE BOOKS BY SUSIE MCIVER

. . .

SUSIE MCIVER

KILLIAN BOOK 1
  My Book

ROWAN BOOK 2
  My Book

ZANE BOOK 3
  My Book

ASH BOOK 5
  <u>My Book</u>

JONAH BOOK 6
  <u>My Book</u>

KANE BOOK 7
  My Book

AUSTIN BOOK 8
  My Book
  LUKE
  My Book
  RYES
  My Book

SOCIAL MEDIA

Newsletter Sign Up http://bit.ly/SusieMcIver_Newsletter

Facebook Page: www.facebook.com/SusieMcIverAuthor/

Facebook Group: www.facebook.com/groups/SusieMcIverAuthor/

Printed in Great Britain
by Amazon